DEAD BY THE OUTLAW'S NOOSE

A MADDIE SWALLOWS MYSTERY
BOOK 8

KAT BELLEMORE

KB PRESS

1

Gunfire. Two shots.

Benji had already been driving slowly along the winding roads of the Colorado mountains, but when we'd had to turn off onto a bumpy dirt road a mile back, we'd been forced to a crawl. I was exhausted from the drive and anxious to get to our hotel, but after hearing those gunshots...I was suddenly no longer in a hurry. Getting stuck in the middle of a shootout was hardly the way to start our honeymoon.

I squinted, trying to see through the trees. The forest was dense, and if the shooter was hiding in there, it would be impossible to tell.

It turned out that the trees weren't where our attention needed to be.

We had just reached a bend in the road when a man stepped out in front of us. He held out a hand like he was a construction worker, though he wore chaps and a cowboy hat.

Benji, whose sole focus was on avoiding the numerous potholes, didn't notice the man, who was calmly standing there, smiling, fully expecting us to stop.

"Benji," I squealed.

My husband glanced up, then slammed his foot on the brake. We skidded to a stop, bouncing off one of the potholes that Benji had been working so hard to avoid.

My breaths came quick and heavy, and I held onto the dashboard.

"What is someone doing in the middle of the road?" Benji asked, his breathing as labored as my own. "I could have killed him."

As if in response to Benji's question, enthusiastic booing punctuated the air, and a cowboy on a horse appeared at the bend, racing as if his life depended on it. He was dressed all in black, and a bandana covered the bottom half of his face. His horse carried three canvas bags with large dollar signs printed on the sides.

"That's the outlaw of Dusty Ridge," Benji whispered, his eyes lighting up in excitement.

As the cowboy raced past us, we made eye contact, and he tipped his hat.

Okay, a polite outlaw.

Dusty Ridge.

It wasn't exactly the romantic honeymoon destination I'd had in mind, but that was partly my fault. Things had gotten busy, with my dad being murdered and all that, and I was still in my sappy *I don't care as long as I'm with you* phase. So, I had told Benji that he could choose where we spent our honeymoon.

I was starting to care, now that we were arriving at the small Colorado town of Dusty Ridge, known for its classic Western movie sets, midday shootouts, and late-afternoon bank robberies.

I turned to Benji, who was leaning over the steering wheel, craning his neck, as if he could see through the trees that surrounded us. His ginormous grin told me that even though we hadn't checked into our hotel yet, he was in heaven.

I slipped back into my *I don't care as long as I'm with you* laissez-faire attitude, because seeing Benji this happy—I really didn't care.

And who knew, maybe it would turn out that Dusty Ridge was the most romantic place that Benji could have chosen. If I were honest with myself, I wouldn't mind seeing Benji in a cowboy hat and tight jeans. In fact, the more I thought about it, the more I realized the potential this honeymoon held.

We had to wait another minute or two, but then the cowboy in front of the car waved us forward, and we rumbled along the dirt road that led into town. True to the town's name, dust swirled around the car as we drove, so much so that I could taste it, even with the windows up.

When we rounded the corner, my eyes widened and

Benji's smile grew. If I hadn't known better—which I didn't —I'd have said this town hadn't changed at all since the 1800s. Wooden storefronts with plank walkways stretched in front of us. To the right of us was a barber, a pharmacy, a bank, and the sheriff's station. Further ahead on the left was a fire station with a single fire engine, a bakery, and a two-story saloon.

The car lumbered forward, and Benji eventually slowed to a stop. He turned to me, his smile having never faded. "So, what do you think?"

I lowered my window and stuck my head out. A cool breeze washed over me—a stark contrast to the heat of New Mexico.

From Benji's expression, I could tell that he expected I had fallen in love with this town as much as he already had. It was funny, because Benji knew me better than anyone else in the world, with the exception of my kids. And he honestly believed this old Western town would be my idea of the perfect honeymoon.

The jury was still out on that verdict, but if Benji was so sure I'd love it, I was willing to give it a chance.

"It's beautiful here," I said, taking in the mountains that surrounded us. "And there is plenty to keep us enter-tained. As long as the shootouts remain fictional. After the wedding we had, we don't need any more dead bodies."

Benji gave me a quick kiss. "I couldn't agree more." And then he popped the trunk and jumped out of the car.

"Shouldn't we wait until we get to the hotel to unload?"

I asked. I hadn't brought an excessive amount of clothes, but it was enough to fill two suitcases. I had wanted to ensure I had the right items for the right weather.

"We're already here," Benji said, setting one of my suitcases on the planked walkway. He nodded toward the saloon.

I blinked. "We're staying...in a bar?" It looked nice enough—it seemed it had been renovated recently and had that 'now open for business' kind of look about it. But it wasn't exactly what I'd had in mind for our honeymoon.

"It's a saloon, not a bar," Benji said. "And we're staying in the suite above it. Very exclusive. We'll have the entire second floor to ourselves." He walked back to the trunk to retrieve the other two bags. "There was availability above the sheriff's office, but the rooms are a lot smaller. I thought the splurge was worth it."

My darling husband had splurged for the saloon suite. Maybe it would be better than I was imagining it to be.

Husband. I still wasn't quite used to calling him that, but I hoped the novelty never wore off.

"Sounds wonderful," I said, stepping out of the car. I took my suitcase from his hand, and as I lugged it toward the front doors, a woman stepped out. She was in full saloon attire, donning a red sequined dress with black lace and a matching feathered hat.

She gave me a warm smile. "Welcome to Dusty Ridge. You must be Maddison."

"I am," I said, returning her smile. "And this is my husband, Benji."

The woman nodded, as if she'd expected as much. "Congratulations on your recent marriage." She motioned to a young man who stood behind her, hidden by the old-fashioned swinging doors.

The young man stepped through the doors and nodded toward the suitcases. "May I?"

Dusty Ridge was more refined than I had given it credit for. "Yes. Thank you."

The young man took our three suitcases and disappeared back inside.

"I hope you'll find your accommodations satisfactory," the woman said, turning back to us. "My name is Amelia Bloomfield—but you can call me Amy. If you need anything at all, you just let me know, and I'll take care of it."

"Thank you so much, Amy," I said, immediately liking her.

She gestured toward the saloon. "Let's get you two checked in, and I'll show you to your room."

Benji took my hand and squeezed it, his excitement palpable. As we followed Amy inside, he leaned in and whispered in my ear, "After she shows us where our room is, I had something special in mind. If you're up to it, of course. I know long drives make you tired."

A shiver of anticipation ran up my spine.

"Oh, yeah?" I said, my tone teasing. "What did you have in mind?"

"Visiting the movie sets on the other side of town," he said. "I only caught a glimpse of them on our way in, but did I tell you that *Six Shots to Sundown* and *Deadwood Sky* were both filmed right here in Dusty Ridge?"

I looked for any hint that Benji was kidding, but he looked like a boy who had woken up early on Christmas morning and was just waiting for permission to burst down the stairs and see what Santa had brought him.

I had known that Benji had enjoyed watching old Westerns with his dad growing up, but I hadn't realized just how much he'd enjoyed them until now.

"I think I can muster up enough energy to walk over there with you," I said with a laugh. Anything else I'd thought Benji had in mind could wait.

Amy walked behind the bar, which apparently doubled as the check-in counter, to code our keycards. "Not that I was eavesdropping," Amy said, picking up a pamphlet from beside her, "but if you're interested in the history of our town, and the movies that have been filmed here, you'll find this worth a read." She handed it to Benji. "We also have an indoor museum with real props from the movies. You won't find any replicas here—our pride wouldn't allow it."

"And for those that might not be as into that sort of thing," she continued, handing me a different pamphlet, "we do offer spa services." She gave me a wink, like she knew what I'd been thinking.

I wasn't sure what about me said I would prefer a spa to a museum, but Amy had read me wrong. Was I into cowboy movies? No, not really. But I loved history, and I loved museums—I could get lost in plaques for hours. I also really loved movies. I'd always wanted to visit an active movie set and hoped I still might someday. For right now, this might be the closest I was going to get.

"Thank you," I said, folding the pamphlet and slipping it into my purse. I didn't want to hurt her feelings by appearing ungrateful.

Amy seemed pleased with herself for a job well done, handed us our keycards, and then led us to an elevator in the back.

"This is a private elevator," Amy said, glancing over her shoulder at us. "You are the only ones who can access it, and it will take you directly to your room. Don't worry, there is a privacy door that you can close so that if you need anything from us, we aren't walking in unannounced." She gave us a wink as she swiped our keycard. The elevator doors instantly opened.

I knew I shouldn't be embarrassed by the innuendo, but I couldn't help the blush that crept into my cheeks. "Thank you for all your help," I said, pushing Benji into the elevator and hitting the 'close door' button. "I'm sure everything will be just perfect."

"You'll find a menu in your room," Amy continued,

even as the doors were closing. "Your breakfast is complimenta—"

The elevator door cut off the rest of her sentence.

Benji glanced at me, an amused eyebrow raised. "What was all that about?"

"Sorry," I said. "I get weird when other people make a big deal about newlywed couples and...stuff."

He laughed and pulled me in for a kiss. "What if we were the ones who made it weird for *her*?"

Our lips lingered, and then I pulled back, scrunching my nose. "Then I'd never be able to look her in the eye if I needed so much as an extra blanket."

Benji smirked. The elevator doors opened, and we stepped out into the Saloon Suite.

"You're sure you want to run out to that movie set right away?" I asked, taking in the large room. A dining area sat to our left, complete with a table filled with chocolates and sparkling cider. A king-size bed sat in the middle of the room with rose petals sprinkled over it. If we wanted to take in the sunset later, a private balcony welcomed us. And of course it was all Western themed, complete with a cowboy boot clock on the wall.

"I suppose we could rest up first," Benji said, scooping me up in his arms.

I squealed as he tossed me onto the bed.

I could get used to living in the Wild West.

2

It felt a lot later than it was when Benji and I finally emerged from the Saloon Suite and stepped into the elevator. I stifled a yawn as it reached the main floor.

Amy glanced our way when we stepped out, and she gave a wave. Benji took the opportunity to grab my hand, pull me into a dramatic dip, and then give me a giant kiss.

"Oh, come on," I said when he pulled me back to my feet. My face burned with both embarrassment and attraction to my husband, and I hoped the blush wasn't obvious. "I know you think you're making it weird for Amy, but honestly, look at her face—she's delighted."

Benji glanced over to the bar and couldn't ignore Amy's large smile. "Yeah, my plan seems to have backfired." It was cute how disappointed he sounded.

"Think of how lonely it must be, living in a place like this," I said, taking his hand and pulling him toward the front door. "Are there any actual residents in this town, or is everyone that Amy interacts with either a co-worker or a tourist?"

My eyes were still blurry from sleep, and I rubbed them, remembering a moment too late that I was still wearing mascara. Amy might think she knew what had happened up there in the bedroom, but little did she know that Benji had been spot on when he'd said that long car drives made me sleepy. Sometime after my fortieth birthday, I had regressed into a toddler, and I had just taken a three-hour nap to recuperate from the busy day. That had been a mistake, as I was now more tired than before.

I glanced up at Benji with a pleading look and pulled a tissue from my purse. "Help, please."

He smiled and used it to wipe away whatever mascara I had inadvertently smeared. "Good as new."

This was what true romance looked like. Sure, passionate kisses were nice. But having a man who looked at my mascara-smudged face with love and helped wipe the smears away? That was something special.

"Food first, or movie sets?" I asked, pushing through the saloon doors.

My stomach said food, but I had made Benji wait long enough for his *Six Shots to Sundown* adventure. Dinner could wait.

Before Benji could answer, I pulled him to the right. "You're right, we should go see the movie sets first."

Benji's eyes lit up. "Really?"

I nodded. "Absolutely."

He kissed my forehead. "You really do love me."

"I married you, didn't I?"

There weren't many people out on Main Street, but those we saw were taking pictures with various props that had been placed around town for photo ops. One man had his head and hands stuck in a stockade, a grim look on his face, like he was being punished.

"I think this town is pretty cool," I whispered to Benji, "but you are not getting a picture of me in that thing. I refuse to be that kind of tourist."

"Absolutely not," Benji agreed.

We rounded the corner, and I could see the movie sets in the distance. This area of town looked awfully deserted, though. The only person in the vicinity was a man wearing a backwards baseball cap who was trimming some grass on the side of the road.

Benji didn't seem to notice and was thrilled just to be there. "You okay if we're the kind of tourists who get their picture taken with fake backdrops?"

Before I could answer, the man with the trimmer noticed us and hurried over. "You must have missed the sign. The museum is closed for the evening. You can come back in the morning. It opens at ten a.m."

"Can we at least look at the movie sets and come back tomorrow for the museum?" Benji asked, already trying to step around the man. He really wanted to see those sets.

"The sets are a part of the museum," the man said.

Now that I looked, I saw the barriers that had been strategically placed so that tourists were herded through the museum before they were allowed to see the outdoor exhibits.

It was my fault we'd arrived after closing—me and my three-hour nap. The instant I'd hit the bed, I had crawled under the covers, and Benji and I had fallen asleep together.

Benji tried to hide his disappointment. "Tomorrow it is, then."

The man noticed Benji's slumped shoulders and said, "I do know somewhere else you could visit, and not many people know it's here. Hidden in plain sight, if you will. But you have to follow my instructions exactly."

That sounded ominous, but if there was a time to have an adventure, this was it. Besides, I owed Benji.

"Okay," I said, pulling out my phone and tapping on the Notes icon. "What have you got for us?"

The man smiled, and it made me uneasy. Like he was playing a prank on us. "You're going to go back out on the main road," he started.

When I didn't start typing right away, he pointedly glanced at my phone. Right.

Main road.

"Go until the fire station, and then turn right. You'll then take the next left. Three buildings up on the right-hand side of the road is a hotel. Don't go through the main door. On the side of the building is a small set of stairs that leads down to a green door. That's the one you want."

Right at fire station.

Next left.

Third building on the right—hotel.

Green door on the side.

I glanced up from my phone. "Where exactly does this lead us?"

The man had already turned his back on us and was walking away with his trimmer slung over his shoulder.

Benji's gaze followed the groundskeeper before it returned to me. "What do you think? Should we do it?"

Even though I hesitated, I knew exactly what the answer had to be.

"Of course we should," I said, taking his hand. "Otherwise, we'll always wonder what was behind the green door. We're not the *photo-op* or *let's hang out on the beach all day* tourists. We're the *let's get murdered behind a green door* tourists. The ones in the horror movie that everyone is wondering why they're going into the creepy basement during a power outage."

Benji laughed and squeezed my hand. "That we are."

"First direction is to get back to the main road," I said. The sun was starting to lower, casting an orange and yellow hue over the trees. We had beautiful sunsets in New Mexico, but we didn't have anything like these trees or mountains. I loved it. "Dusty Ridge was a good pick," I said, glancing at Benji. "I can't think of a better place for our honeymoon."

He looked down, and his eyes crinkled with his smile. "I know you were skeptical when I told you where we were going, but I'm glad you like it."

My lips parted in surprise. "You knew?"

He laughed. "Of course I did. But believe it or not, I really did think this through. I know that you dislike crowds and love nature, but you also avoid camping and prefer to be close to civilization. You enjoy history and movies and are always up for an adventure." He pointed to the list of instructions on my phone. "Case in point."

"Combine all that with your love of Western movies, and this seemed like the perfect place," I finished for him.

Benji nodded. "So, you're happy with my choice?" He still seemed unsure, like maybe I was only saying what I thought he wanted to hear.

"I love...it." My words slowed when my eye caught movement in the trees to the left of us.

"What's wrong?" Benji asked, trying to see where my gaze had landed.

I squinted, wondering if it was just shadows playing tricks on me. Because what I thought I was seeing would have been crazy. Even in a town like this.

"Nothing," I said, turning back to him. "My eyes are messing with me."

Benji didn't dismiss it so easily. As he'd just proved, he knew me.

His gaze scanned the trees where I'd been looking. "Did you think you saw a person in the trees?" Benji asked, his words slow.

"Yes, but really, let's go find whatever mysterious place the groundskeeper wanted to send us to. That sounds much more fun than—"

"And was that person alive?" he interrupted.

I sucked in a quick breath. "No, not likely."

"Because he was hanging from a tree."

I stayed silent, not wanting to answer his question. Because my eyes hadn't been playing tricks on me—Benji was seeing the same thing I was.

"Maddie?" Benji prodded, his gaze intense.

When I gave a slight nod, he dropped my hand and sprinted toward the trees.

No. This was not happening again.

Another reason I had told Benji he could choose our honeymoon destination was so that I wouldn't jinx it. If I had chosen, a body would have been guaranteed to show up. But not if Benji chose.

Which was why there wasn't a figure hanging from a tree, a noose around his neck.

Benji approached the figure and immediately tried to find a way to reach the rope, but the branch was too high. He paced with quick and frantic steps, muttering to himself as he tried to think of a solution.

"Benji," I said, placing a hand on his arm. "It's no use. He's already dead."

Benji stopped mid-step. "Do you recognize him?"

I hadn't wanted to look at the figure—that would mean I had to admit he was real. But I turned my attention to the man. I didn't recognize the face, but I did recognize the clothes. I reached out and touched the sleeve's cuff.

"It's the outlaw," I whispered. "The one who robbed the bank."

3

I backed away from the body and pulled out my phone to dial 911, only to realize that my phone was dead. Funny that I hadn't noticed until now. Normally I would have already called to check on my kids a couple of times. Of course, Lilly had told me not to call, so I supposed I was keeping my promise.

"Why does this always happen?" I whispered, close to tears. "We barely made it a few hours."

Benji rested a hand on my arm. "At least we found him, instead of a family with kids accidentally stumbling upon the body."

"True," I said. "I would have been okay if the groundskeeper had found him, though."

"But what if this was his friend? At least with us, it isn't likely to scar us for the rest of our lives."

Benji had a point.

"Okay, so do we track down whatever law enforcement this town has and hope no one else finds the body while we're gone?" I asked. "Or do we stay here and call 911? We'll have to use your phone, though—mine is dead."

"In a place like this?" Benji said. "It will be better to report is to local law enforcement. I saw the sheriff's office when we drove into town."

I honestly didn't know how helpful small-town cops would be in a place like this, but it was worth a try. "I'll leave a marker by the tree line to make it easier to find," I said. I looked around and saw a large rock that looked suspiciously like a skull. That wasn't comforting. I picked it up and held it up for Benji to see. "This place has some bad juju."

He grimaced. "Yes, it does."

I moved the skull rock closer to the road, and then after a quick glance around, ensuring that no one else was in the vicinity, Benji and I hurried back to the main road.

The sheriff's office wasn't far, and it looked exactly how you'd expect an old Western sheriff's office to look. A wooden rocking chair sat on the walkway in front of the window, and I wondered if the sheriff ever sat in that chair as he kept an eye on the town. Of course, whether this was an actual functioning sheriff's office was another matter, and one that we hadn't considered. Everything else in town seemed to be functional, but you never knew with a tourist town like this.

Benji pushed the front door open, and I suddenly had my doubts—it felt like we'd stepped into a tourism office rather than anything that had to do with law enforcement. Brochures sat on the front counter, advertising the museum and local ghost town tours.

"I don't know if we're in the right place," I whispered.

Benji hesitated, like he was also unsure, but he stepped forward and hit a bell that sat on the counter.

A tall, skinny man stepped out. He wore a big hat and a small vest, a sheriff's star pinned on his chest. All he was missing was a mustache. Even without it, I could have sworn he'd stepped right out of a movie.

"Good evening," the sheriff said. His voice was far lower than I had expected. "Welcome to Dusty Ridge's sheriff's office, where outlaws don't stand a chance."

It had been obviously rehearsed, and from the tired tone, the sheriff had said it twelve too many times that day.

"Good evening," I said, stepping up beside Benji. I hesitated. "Are you by any chance... I don't know the best way to ask this...but are you an actual sheriff with the ability to process a crime scene or arrest someone...or are you....well....not..."

The sheriff's demeanor shifted, and he held up a hand to stop me, which I was enormously grateful for. I had been rambling, not wanting to offend him if he was legitimate law enforcement, but also not wanting to get too far ahead of myself if he was merely an actor.

"I'm going to stop you right there," he said. "Are you here to report a crime?"

We knew nothing about what had happened to the poor outlaw or how he'd ended up in that tree, and I was unsure how to answer the question.

"Report a dead body is more like it," Benji said.

The sheriff's eyes widened, and he held up a finger. "You stay there." And then he disappeared into the back of the sheriff's station.

A few moments later, a short woman with long red hair walked in from the back, her expression both quizzical and concerned. Freckles covered most of her face, making her appear younger than she likely was.

"You're here to report a body?" she asked.

"Yes," Benji said.

The woman approached us and stuck out a hand. "I'm Sheriff McKnight. Pleased to make your acquaintance."

Benji couldn't hide his shock as he took the woman's hand. She then offered it to me, and I smiled.

"You're the sheriff of Dusty Ridge?" I glanced over at the tall man who had initially greeted us. His head poked out from the back, like he wasn't supposed to be there but he didn't want to miss anything.

"I'm sorry," Benji said, stumbling over his words. "I didn't mean to be so surprised, I just—"

Sheriff McKnight merely smiled. "It's okay. I get that reaction a lot. But honestly, I don't have a lot of interaction with the general public. Folks in town know where to come if they have a problem, but Deputy Steve Sanders over there," she nodded behind her, "he's the face of the office. Women weren't sheriff back in the 1800s, and the mayor likes us to be as historically accurate as possible—otherwise, he gets an earful from the history buffs who come and visit. So, for the tourists, Deputy Sanders plays sheriff, and I get to actually do my job. I kind of like it that way." Her smile dipped. "But what is this about you finding a body?"

Benji and I shared anxious looks.

"He's hanging from a noose in the trees near the museum," I said.

"Hanging," Sheriff McKnight said, the word drawn out.

Benji nodded. "From a noose. And—" He hesitated. "He was still in costume."

The sheriff's breath caught. "You mean, he's a local."

"We believe he's the outlaw from your show earlier today," I said. "He was wearing the black cowboy outfit."

This got a bigger reaction from the sheriff.

She sprinted to the back of the office. When she returned, she held a serrated knife. She wore a grim expression as she swung open the counter door. She already wore a holster, but rather than looking comical on her short stature, it made her look tough. Like she was ready to take on anyone that stood in her way. Before leading us out the front door, she turned back to her deputy.

"Steve, not a word of this gets out until I get some confirmation on what's going on, do you understand?"

The deputy nodded fervently. "Yes, ma'am."

"I'm serious, Steve. Not a word to anyone, including those boys of yours."

Steve seemed to have lost his voice for a moment, likely thinking that his 'boys' hadn't counted. I was sure he'd previously made the mistake of thinking they hadn't counted and gotten in trouble for it then, too.

"Yes, ma'am," he said again, though this time his voice didn't hold quite as much power as it had.

She spun back around and pushed open the front door, leaving Benji and me scrambling to catch up.

"How long ago did you find him?" Sheriff McKnight asked, a good three paces in front of us. In spite of her shorter legs, she had no problem with speed.

"About twenty minutes," I said.

"Anyone else see him?"

I shook my head, even though she couldn't see the movement. "No, we're the only ones, thank goodness. We know how traumatic it can be to see someone in a state like that."

The sheriff paused and glanced back. "You seem to have experience with this kind of thing. What do you two do for work?"

I glanced at Benji before saying, "I'm a psychologist, and I've worked as a consultant with our own local sheriff in several murder cases. I have more experience than I wish I had."

Calling myself a consultant was a bit of a stretch, but the last thing we needed was Sheriff McKnight thinking we had anything to do with this death.

My answer seemed to satisfy the sheriff, though, and she nodded before turning and resuming her quick pace.

"We're lucky to have you, then," she said.

My chest tightened.

"I don't think you'll need us, apart from showing you where the man died," Benji quickly said. He must have sensed the immediate panic I'd felt at the thought of assisting the sheriff in her investigation. "I doubt it was foul play."

Sheriff McKnight stopped mid-step and spun to face us. "Jeremy did not commit suicide, if that is what you're suggesting. He wouldn't do that. Which means we are dealing with either an accident or murder."

I doubted the young man had tripped and landed inside a noose that just so happened to be hanging from the tree, but I could tell this was very personal for the sheriff, and I kept my mouth shut, merely nodding in agreement.

"He's in the grove of trees directly across from the museum entrance," Benji said, his voice quiet. He stepped around the sheriff to lead the way.

The sheriff straightened, seeming embarrassed at her

emotional outburst, and followed. As quick as she had been before, her steps had slowed, and she no longer seemed to be in a hurry.

But when Benji and I arrived at the spot where we'd discovered the man, there was no body.

And no noose.

4

Sheriff McKnight looked at us, her gaze expectant. "So, where is he?"

Benji and I shared glances, and the sheriff didn't need to ask what it meant.

"You lost him. Or you thought you saw something that never existed in the first place." She let out a frustrated sigh and then turned away. "Please enjoy your vacation. And do me a favor—cross the sheriff's office off your list of places to visit."

"We didn't imagine it," I said, hurrying after the sheriff. "He really was there. Maybe we got the wrong spot. All these trees look the same. Maybe it was further down the tree line."

I knew it wasn't—the skull rock was still sitting there where I'd placed it, mocking me.

Sheriff McKnight's footsteps slowed, and she glanced

back at me. "Look, this town seems to have an effect on people. Some say it's haunted, I say that people get lost in the ambience. It's an old Western town where generations of people have lived and died—we have local folks whose ancestors actually settled the place. We've tried to keep Dusty Ridge in its original state, and sometimes that messes with people's heads."

"You mean, others have seen dead bodies here?" Benji asked, his gaze returning to the trees. He knew as well as I did that we weren't at the wrong place. Unless there were multiple rocks that looked like skulls in these woods. Somehow, I doubted it.

The sheriff gave a curt nod. "Dead bodies...ghosts.... none of it is real, though. We haven't had a murder in this town since 1963."

"It looked so real," I murmured.

"It always does," Sheriff McKnight said. "The thing is, whenever someone reports a murder, it has always been with a gun or a noose—your classic Western weapons of choice. And the fact that you saw someone who was dressed in cowboy attire... Well, your imagination got the best of you."

Maybe it had. I was suddenly questioning everything we'd done that day.

"Do people ever see ghosts of groundskeepers?" I glanced around, looking for the man who had given us those ridiculous directions.

He was nowhere to be seen.

Sheriff McKnight released a quick laugh. "No. You must have met Chuck. I saw him head off in his truck just as we got here."

At least *he* was real.

I glanced at Benji, questioning. Was it possible we had both seen something that hadn't been real? It seemed unlikely, but I supposed it could happen. I'd read a book about a married couple who had a shared psychotic disorder where the wife had had delusions and was able to convince her husband that he was experiencing the same thing.

And I had noticed the body first.

Did that make me the psychotic one in our relationship?

"I'm sorry that we've dragged you out here for nothing," Benji said. "It seems we've fallen victim to the ghosts of this town."

Sheriff McKnight gave us a kind smile. "It happens to the best of us, and I'd rather ghosts than an actual body."

As would I.

So, why couldn't I shake the feeling that what Benji and I had seen had been very much real?

The sheriff gave us a wave of farewell and then disappeared into the encroaching darkness, hurrying back the way we had come.

"What do you think?" I asked Benji as we watched her retreating figure.

Benji remained silent as he turned back to the trees,

his gaze searching, as if the body and the noose would suddenly reappear.

"We saw it," I said. "You tried to get the body down. I touched the fabric on his clothes. We didn't imagine that. Right?"

Benji nodded, the movement slow. "It wasn't a ghost. Someone must have cut him down after we left. It's too dark now to look for drag marks in the dirt. Let's come back tomorrow, bright and early. Before that groundskeeper—Chuck—shows up for work."

I glanced at him. "You think it was him who cut down the body?"

Benji lifted a shoulder. "Maybe. He could have seen us examining it and then got rid of it before we came back with the sheriff."

I glanced at the trees, frowning. "If we didn't imagine the body, then the two options for how the outlaw died are murder and suicide. If it was murder, why would someone kill him with a noose? Hanging someone is not easy, and it's very public. It doesn't make sense to murder him that way, only to then go to the trouble of making the body disappear."

"And if it was suicide?" Benji asked.

"Then why would someone take the body, rather than report it like we did? It doesn't make sense either."

"You're right," Benji said. "There's no good answer. Let's try to get a good night's sleep and come back in the morning. Maybe we'll find something."

As Benji turned away, me still glancing over my shoulder, ensuring the outlaw truly wasn't there, I remembered there was a third option. "What if the sheriff was right, and it really was a ghost?" I realized how crazy that sounded and clarified, "Not a real ghost, of course. But something that was intended to make us think it was."

Benji raised a quizzical eyebrow. "You're buying the sheriff's ghost story?"

I shook my head. "More like a prank. A fake body that the locals hang up once in a while, in various locations, to spook tourists and get them to tell stories. But most people don't choose to get up close and personal. Normal people run away. And they tell their friends about the haunted town of Dusty Ridge. Which, in turn, gets more tourists flocking to the town to see if they can spot a ghost."

I liked that explanation better than thinking I was psychotic and had taken Benji along for the ride.

Benji's lips twitched up at the edges. "You think they were Scooby-Doo-ing us."

"Yes, exactly."

When I was a kid, something I'd always liked about Scooby-Doo was that I always knew, no matter how scared the gang was, that in the end, the ghost would be a guy in a sheet or a projection on a wall.

Ghosts weren't real.

I really hoped that was what was going on here.

"That means that the fake body is likely to pop up in some other part of town in a couple of days, to scare some other poor soul," Benji said. "And the sheriff—if she's an actual sheriff—continues the story about the haunted town of the Old West."

"It's brilliant, really," I said, feeling much better about everything. It was the explanation that made the most sense, and it meant no dead bodies.

And no murder.

THE NEXT MORNING, rather than waking up bright and early to catch a murderer, Benji and I slept in. We had an amazing breakfast of biscuits and gravy brought up to our room, and around ten o'clock, we lazily made our way out into the sun.

"When is the next bank robbery?" I asked Benji as we walked down the wooden walkway, taking in the scenery. Now that I'd gotten over my initial shock that we were staying in a saloon for our honeymoon, the little town of Dusty Ridge was growing on me.

Benji's eyes lit up in excitement. "You want to watch the show?"

I laughed and nodded. "Yes, I do. And I want to visit the museum and see the old movie sets. And go on the ghost town tour. I want to do it all."

Benji could barely contain his excitement. "And the train museum? Trains played such an important role in the development of the West. They have a steam engine on display that we can go inside of and—"

I stopped him with a kiss. "Yes, I even want to do the train museum."

Maybe this wasn't the honeymoon I had expected, but it was sure a lot more interesting than lying out on a beach somewhere—I doubted Hawaii had ghosts and bank robberies.

"Shall we start with the museum?" I asked. My mind drifted to the previous evening. Even though I'd managed to convince Benji that the dead outlaw was part of a town-wide prank, part of me wanted to start with the old movie sets to prove to myself that that was all it had been.

Benji grinned as he took my hand and pulled me down the walkway. "The museum sounds perfect."

As Benji told me all about the various movies that had been filmed here, I absentmindedly nodded, distracted by the sheriff's office on the other side of the street. As we passed by, I looked for movement. I didn't know what I expected to see—maybe Sheriff McKnight sprinting across the street to tell us that we were right, that we had seen something. That someone was dead.

The door to the office opened, but it wasn't the sheriff. A family of four exited, and the two small children excitedly chattered, pointing to the honorary sheriff badges pinned to their chests.

It seemed that maybe Benji was right and Sheriff McKnight wasn't a real sheriff at all. Just another attraction in a dying town that had turned to tourism to try to survive.

Benji and I rounded the corner at the end of the street and made our way toward the museum. I couldn't allow us to just pass by the wooded area where we'd seen the body, though. Not without looking.

"I know we determined that last night was a prank, and we want to just enjoy our honeymoon," I said. "But humor me. Can we at least look for any signs that there was a noose on that tree or a body was moved?"

Benji gave me a patient smile. "Even if we found evidence of a rope or drag marks, it wouldn't prove anything. The fake body would have probably been dragged through the dirt, same as a real one, and the rope would have been real regardless."

He had a point on both counts.

"Okay," I said, relenting. "You're right. I need to let it go."

With a quick kiss on his cheek, I pulled him toward the museum.

"Hey," someone called from behind us. We stopped and glanced back. There was Chuck, the groundskeeper, leaning on a shovel. "I hear you found a body last night."

Looked like we had found our prankster.

"Turns out we didn't," Benji said with a smile.

"Guess that means you didn't go on my little adventure last night," Chuck said.

"Not yet, but we're still here for a few days."

Chuck gave a small nod. "Today's just as good a day as

any." And then he turned away, slinging the shovel over his shoulder, and wandered off.

"He totally did it," I whispered.

Benji smiled. "He certainly did."

He opened the museum door for me, then followed me into what might have been a lobby if it weren't so small. It was more like a hallway with a bench that took up half the space. A payment desk sat in front of us, and then to our left, the space opened up to the museum.

A man and woman stood by the desk, arguing. Instead of the quiet that one comes to expect of such a place, we were thrown into the chaos of the moment, and I wondered if we should come back later.

"How could you have not noticed that it was missing?" the man asked. He was an older gentleman with gray hair and a beard. "I noticed the moment I walked through this morning."

"Because I'm not here to just take in the exhibits," the woman snapped. She seemed to be around the same age as the gentleman. Her hair was pinned up the way my mom liked it, and she was wearing a business suit. "I was here early, rearranging the pistols to make room for the new one that was donated last week."

"Was it here when you left last night?"

The woman waved a hand through the air, like it was a silly question. "I don't know. Maybe. But honestly, it could have just been misplaced. We've been rearranging a lot of the items lately, and the volunteers here don't always know where things go." She gave the man a pointed look—I had a feeling he was one of those volunteers.

"I know far more about this museum than you do, Peggy. Why else did the board ask for my help when creating the plaques? As an official museum consultant, I'm telling you that you need to do a better job cataloguing our items. Maybe then you'd have noticed when one of them was stolen."

"We'll have to agree to disagree," Peggy said. "When I find it later today, you'll see that it was merely misplaced by one of our well-intentioned volunteers. A rope is not worth stealing. There are other items here that are far more valuable, and they weren't touched."

"It wasn't as heavily guarded as the other items. No locks and no alarms," the man said, running his fingers through his hair, obviously frustrated. "The thief could probably sell it online for a good amount if they could prove it had been used in *Deadwood Sky*."

"Are you hearing this?" I asked, turning to Benji in alarm.

His jaw had slackened, and he gave a slow nod. "Yeah. It sounds like the museum is missing a noose."

5

"I have to agree with Peggy," Benji murmured. "Why would someone steal a noose?"

That was a very good question. If they had simply wanted to hang the man, any old rope would do. No need to go to the trouble of stealing one. And why hang him at all? It was such an archaic, and brutal, way to kill someone.

"Maybe it wasn't premeditated," I said, my mind running through all possibilities. "They get into an altercation, and the killer decides that the outlaw has to go. He knows there's a noose in here, and he runs in and grabs it."

"And what, the outlaw just stood there, waiting for the killer to come back, place the noose around his neck, and then figure out how to string him up in the trees?"

Benji had a good point.

"It could work if the outlaw was already dead and the killer needed a way to make it look like a suicide."

Benji scrunched his forehead. He wasn't buying it. "That scenario has already been done countless times in movies, and it never works. The medical examiner is always able to tell that the victim died before they were strung up."

"But our killer wouldn't have been thinking things through rationally—he would have panicked."

Benji folded his arms. "Why are you assuming it was a man who was the killer? It could have been a woman."

"Women are naturally smaller than men—it would have had to be a very strong woman."

He raised a shoulder in concession.

Someone cleared their throat, and Benji and I glanced over, having momentarily forgotten that we weren't alone. Both Peggy and the man were staring at us, their eyebrows raised.

"I'm sorry, who are you?" Peggy asked. The way she was looking at us—it was like she was challenging us to lie.

So, I didn't.

I gave her a warm smile and took Benji's hand in mine. "Hi, my name is Maddison, and this is my husband, Benji. We're here on our honeymoon. Just arrived last night."

Peggy grunted. "Where are you staying?"

"The saloon," I answered, never letting my smile drop.

The man gave a nod, like he already knew this information. "It's true. Amy checked them in last night."

Peggy's gaze never left us. "So, why is a newlywed

couple theorizing that someone was murdered with a stolen movie prop?"

The man turned his attention back to Peggy. "I thought you said it wasn't stolen."

"Of course it was stolen," Peggy snapped. "But I can't have you telling everyone and sending them into a panic that staged bank robberies are not the only crime taking place in their town. Now we have props missing, and this couple seems to think we also have a murder on our hands." She turned back to Benji and me. "You didn't answer my question. Who are you really?"

I hesitated, and I was saved from answering when the man spoke up on our behalf.

"Peggy, I'm telling you, they are staying in the suite at the saloon."

"That doesn't mean they aren't up to something," Peggy said, her gaze never leaving me. It was intense—like, mother-in-law intense.

Benji gave a slight nod, encouraging me to tell them. If we were going to get any useful information, they needed to be able to trust us.

"Assisting in murder investigations is a bit of a specialty of mine," I reluctantly admitted. "I've helped our own local sheriff on a number of occasions."

Peggy folded her arms, her gaze boring into me. I couldn't tell if she believed me or not.

The old man gave us a kind smile. "Sounds like you have a very interesting line of work, Maddison. But what gave you the impression that the noose was stolen in order to kill someone?"

It was Benji who answered this time.

"We believe we saw it last night. In the woods. And there was a man's neck inside it."

"Impossible," Peggy said with a scoff. "There hasn't been a murder in Dusty Ridge since—"

"1963. Yes, we know," I said. "And we didn't want to believe it either. We really are on our honeymoon, and trust me, an unexplainable death is the last thing we want right now. But we know what we saw."

Peggy still didn't seem convinced. "Did you report it to Sheriff McKnight?"

Benji nodded. "Yes, but she didn't believe us either. It didn't help that the dead outlaw had disappeared by the time we returned."

I wished Benji hadn't mentioned that last part—it didn't exactly help with our credibility.

It didn't seem to have mattered, though, because Peggy's face paled, and she looked like she was having trouble breathing. "Outlaw?" she said.

"Yes, the one from your bank robbery yesterday."

She stumbled back into the desk, and I grabbed a chair, but she fell to the ground before I could help her into it. I dropped to her side and was checking her pulse when the door to the museum slammed open.

The next few minutes were a blur.

Chuck bursting through the door, his shovel raised,

then someone grabbing me by the arm and yanking me back.

Pain. A lot of it.

Benji shouting at everyone to calm down.

My vision swam, and I blinked a few times, trying to clear it.

By the time the world stopped spinning, I realized I was lying on the floor.

"What happened?" I asked, trying to sit up. My head was pounding, and I fell back down.

"Stay where you are." Sheriff McKnight's face appeared above me, her features laced with concern. She was kneeling over me and taping a large bandage on my forehead. "You've had a hard knock to the head."

That would explain a lot.

"What happened?" I repeated.

Benji appeared by my side, taking my hand. "How are you feeling?"

"Like my head is about to split open," I said, starting to get annoyed. "Will someone tell me what happened?"

Benji glanced at the sheriff, but when her gaze dropped, he turned back to me. "Chuck had been working outside and glanced in through the window. He saw Peggy on the floor, with you hovering over her, and thought you'd done something to her. He rushed in to pull you off, but he pulled too hard and sent you flying into the desk. Thankfully, Seth," he nodded to the old man, "had enough sense to call Sheriff

McKnight, who, as it turns out, is also the doctor of Dusty Ridge."

I blinked.

"A licensed doctor?"

Sheriff McKnight's lips twitched up at one corner. "Yes, licensed." Her smile dipped as she sat back on her ankles. "You hit your head pretty hard and likely have a concussion. I need you to take it easy for the next couple of days. No strenuous activities, limit screen time, and no caffeine."

I had so many questions, but my head hurt too much to care about any of them.

"Now, I do need to put back on my sheriff hat," she said, glancing behind her.

"What do you mean?" I asked, once again trying to sit up. No one stopped me this time.

Sheriff McKnight turned back to me. "I need to arrest Chuck." And then the sheriff pushed herself up off the floor.

I grabbed her pantleg. "Wait."

With the look she gave me, I quickly let go.

"He attacked you," she said.

"But from the way I understand it, he was trying to protect Peggy, wasn't he? Should he have slowed down and read the situation a bit more closely? Of course. But I don't think he deserves to be in jail for that."

Sheriff McKnight hesitated. I could tell she really didn't want to arrest him, and that said a lot about Chuck as a person. He was liked in this town.

"Has he ever hurt someone before?" I pressed.

The sheriff shook her head.

"There you have it."

Sheriff McKnight studied me for a moment before saying, "Thank you." And then she walked away, presumably to tell Chuck that he was a free man.

I glanced over at Benji and extended my hand to him. "Help a girl up?"

He smiled as he took it and gently helped me to my feet. "What you did just now—it's why I fell in love with you. You've always been so kind. And intuitive. You see straight through to someone's heart, always thinking the best of them. I wouldn't have been able to do it." Benji pulled me in close, his breath tickling my ear. "Chuck rushed past me so fast, I had no time to react. When I saw him grab you..." His voice broke. "Well, it doesn't matter now. Seth helped me block Chuck so he couldn't do more damage than he'd already done."

My head started swimming again, and I swayed, but Benji's arms kept me upright.

Sheriff McKnight returned to us, looking more flustered than ever. "I have to get back to the office. Can I give you a ride back to the saloon?"

"That would be much appreciated." I threw a disappointed glance at the museum. "I was really looking forward to this today."

"It will still be here when you're feeling better," the

sheriff said, then motioned for us to follow her. "Take your time. I don't want you to rush."

Even as she said it, I could tell the sheriff was antsy to get back, her body fidgety, like she couldn't stand still.

"Everything okay, sheriff?" I asked as we followed her out to her squad car.

She glanced back at us. "Of course."

"I suppose Peggy told you about the stolen noose. When it rains, it pours, am I right?"

Sheriff McKnight stopped mid-step and spun back to face me. "Sorry?"

"It's been an eventful day for you, between the incident with Chuck and the noose, and—"

"And a missing person," the sheriff finished for me.

I hadn't known about that last part.

"Say again?" Benji asked. "Someone's missing?"

She nodded slowly. "Yeah. Our outlaw."

6

B enji and I had wanted to believe that the body we'd seen was a prank. It had been easier that way. But the outlaw Benji and I had seen the previous evening was missing. And so was the museum's noose. It couldn't be a coincidence.

"We should retrace our steps from last night," I said, stepping away from Benji. "The longer we wait, the more likely that the evidence disappears."

"Oh no you don't," he said, catching my arm as I stumbled over my own feet. "You need rest. Doctor's orders. And the sheriff's."

If Sheriff McKnight instructed me to do something, but it was medical advice, would I get in trouble with the law for not complying? Her two distinct positions in the town made things a bit muddled for me.

"But the evidence," I protested.

"I'll point the sheriff in the right direction—just as soon as we get you tucked into bed at the hotel."

I wanted to fight it—stuck in our hotel room by myself, while on my honeymoon no less, was not where I wanted to be. But my head pulsed with pain, and I couldn't think of a single good reason I shouldn't be in bed.

"Fine," I grumbled, "but I'm not happy about it."

MY EYELIDS WERE heavy as I awakened. I turned over and pulled the comforter up higher. The hotel room was quiet, which meant that Benji was still gone.

I wondered how long I'd been asleep. Now that I thought about it, I couldn't remember anything after I had collapsed onto the back seat of Sheriff McKnight's squad car.

That was concerning.

My eyes still closed, I reached out, patting the bed beside me as I blindly searched for my phone. Nothing but blanket. I opened one eye, spotted my purse on the nightstand, and moved to grab it. I immediately regretted the movement. My arm shot back and I cradled my head, praying for the pounding to stop.

It took me another moment before I could make another attempt. This time, I managed to hook a finger around the purse's strap and pull it onto the bed with me. As I fumbled around in my purse for my phone, I glanced at the bedside clock.

3:50

I had slept far longer than I had intended. After a quick glance at my phone, I saw that I also had seven missed calls. All from my mother. It was funny that my children could respect my and Benji's privacy while we were gone for a few days, but my mother was the one who needed a lesson in boundaries. Granted, when I had left home to attend college, my mom and I had barely been on speaking terms. Now, it seemed, she was making up for lost time.

I didn't mind it, usually. In fact, I loved that Flash and Lilly had been able to create the relationship with their grandmother that I'd never had with her. It had been healing for all of us.

That being said, there was a time and place for everything. And her calling me seven times on my honeymoon was not the time for healing.

I was tempted to ignore the missed calls, but what if something was wrong? Maybe she was sick or had landed herself in the hospital. She was getting older—and slower. It wasn't farfetched.

I tapped the call icon and then placed the phone on speaker.

My mom answered after the first ring. "Maddie, what are you doing calling me while on your honeymoon? Are you okay? Did Benji leave you already? I should have known—"

As if she hadn't called me.

"Mom, I'm making sure you're the one who is okay," I interrupted. "You called me seven times."

A pause.

"No, I didn't."

Leave it to my mom to manage to butt dial me seven times in a day. "Check your outgoing calls."

Another pause.

"Oh, it looks like I did call you. I wonder how I managed that."

She'd managed it by not requiring a PIN to access her phone.

"I'm just glad you're safe," I said. "Everyone else doing well?"

My mom harrumphed. "As good as can be expected, without you here. Did you know that your children don't eat vegetables? I cooked dinner for them last night, and Flash wouldn't even touch his salad. Between that and all the screen time, I swear that boy has a death wish."

I smiled. "Either that or he's a teenager."

My mom ignored the statement—she liked believing that she was the one who kept our lives from falling apart. "You and Benji have fun plans for tonight?"

Originally, yeah, we had. After what had happened this morning, though, I wasn't sure what tonight would look like, let alone the rest of the week. I glanced at the clock. "We're playing it by ear. A bank robbery will likely be starting in the next few minutes, so that will be fun." As soon as I said it, however, I realized that there likely wouldn't be a robbery. The outlaw of Dusty Ridge was missing. It was possible that he had an understudy, in case of illness, but did places like this have that kind of thing?

My mom scoffed. "Bank robbery. I like Benji—you know I do—but what was that man thinking? You need romance on a honeymoon, not masked men."

"Or concussions," I muttered.

"What was that?" my mom asked. Thank goodness for her poor hearing.

"Nothing, I have to go, Mom. Thanks for holding down the fort while we're gone."

"Of course. That's what a grandmother does—" Her words cut off as she turned away from the phone. "You can't possibly be finished with your dinner, Flash. I still see broccoli on your plate." A pause. "You know that I don't know the specific vitamins, but it's been proven that if you don't eat your vegetables, you get dumber." A longer pause, and then shuffling. "Okay, but only for a minute. She's on her honeymoon, you know."

"Mom," Flash said, coming on the line. "You need to come save us. Grandma is trying to make us healthy."

I could hear my mom trying to take back control of her phone, but she seemed to be losing the battle.

"Contrary to popular belief, that's not a bad thing," I said. "You and Lilly need to do as she says, okay?"

"But we're adults," he protested. "We're both moving away from home. Surely that's old enough to decide if we want to eat broccoli, or if we want to eat dinner at three-thirty in the afternoon. She says that eating earlier is better for your digestion."

"You're not quite an adult—you graduated early," I reminded him. "And you moving away is all the more reason to do as your grandmother advises. This is hard on her, you know. Once you leave, she won't be able to take care of you anymore."

A grumble. "Fine."

"I love you, Flash, and tell Lilly I love her too."

"Love you."

Just as I was about to end the call, he quickly said, "Wait. Why are you at a saloon?"

My breath caught. "How do you know where I am?"

"You put that app on your phone so you could track where Lilly and I are, and it works both ways."

I should have known that. "And you thought it a good idea to track your mom while she's on her honeymoon?"

"No, I just wanted to know where in Colorado you were. I couldn't remember the name of the town, and Grandma was asking." He paused. "Is everything okay, Mom? You don't usually drink."

"Thank you for your concern, but I just needed a nap is all. Our hotel room is the top floor of the saloon."

"That's so cool," Flash said, sounding envious. "I know it's your honeymoon and everything, but I wish I could have come. I heard you tell Grandma there was going to be a bank robbery."

I laughed. "Next time, I promise I'll bring you."

"Too bad I wasn't recording the conversation so I could remind you of that later," Flash said. A pause. "Can you say it again, please?"

"I promise I'll bring you to Dusty Ridge someday."

I heard my muffled voice replaying in the background, and then Flash talked over it. "Perfect. I got you loud and clear. Now, can you put on Benji? I promise it will be quick, but I have a question about a makeshift repair for my computer desk."

"He's not here right now, but I'm expecting him back any minute," I said. "I'll see if he has time to call you back later tonight."

"Where is he?" Flash asked. "He wouldn't dare go to the bank robbery without you, would he?"

I hesitated, not knowing what to tell Flash—the kids could not know about the missing outlaw. The last thing I needed was for them to get involved.

"No, he just had to run an errand."

"On your honeymoon?"

"Yes. He needed to help someone."

I could hear an argument, and then the phone being transferred to someone else.

"Are you sure everything's okay, Mom?" Lilly asked. "You're at a saloon by yourself while Benji is off doing whatever he's doing. Your wedding had a rocky start, and no one would blame you if—"

"Nothing's wrong," I interrupted, my voice louder than I'd intended. "We are perfectly happy—why does everyone assume that Benji is going to leave me?"

A shocked pause.

"We don't assume that," Lilly said, her voice quiet. "We were just worried, that's all."

I pulled in a long breath. "I'm sorry. It's been a long day. The whole town is a tourist attraction, and it's a little exhausting."

I pushed myself into a sitting position but moved too quickly. I squeezed my eyes shut, waiting for the room to stop spinning. I hated hiding the truth from the kids, but I really couldn't have them getting involved in the outlaw's disappearance.

"Oh, it's one of those kinds of places," Lilly said. "Is that why you were at the sheriff's station last night? And before you get mad, we were only tracking your phone to make sure you made it to Colorado okay. We miss you."

"Yes, the sheriff's station is a part of the tourist trap," I said. "Nothing in this town is real." I could tell that she was still hurt, and I tried my best to smooth things over. "We really are okay."

"Then why won't you tell us what Benji is doing leaving you alone?" she asked. "Who is he helping, and why was it so important that he felt the need to abandon you on your honeymoon?"

It was a fair question, but not one that I wanted to answer.

I rubbed my eyes. "He didn't abandon me—he's

helping the sheriff look for something," I said, trying to be as honest as I could. "It's really not a big deal."

"That's the type of thing that you two normally do together," Lilly pressed. "And normally only for murder investigations."

I blamed myself for my kids' insatiable curiosity—I'd encouraged it. And they weren't going to stop asking questions until I gave them the truth.

"Because I was injured this morning when I fell into a desk at the museum," I admitted. "The sheriff got involved, as she's also the town doctor. I didn't want to tell you, because, frankly, it's embarrassing."

That seemed to do the trick, and Lilly was now more worried about my physical health than Benji's current location. "Are you all right? Did they do any imaging to see if you broke anything? I know that small towns like that don't—"

"A mild concussion is all," I interrupted. "Now, I actually need to get going. I'm on my honeymoon, after all." I paused. "Remember to be good for your grandma."

A grumble. "I'll try, but I can't guarantee that Flash will eat his broccoli."

"I told you, he has a death wish," my mom yelled from somewhere in the distance.

I smiled. Talking to my family had done me some good. Considering the less-than-ideal start to the honeymoon, I'd needed this.

Lilly ended the call, and I pushed myself onto my feet. I

held onto the bed for support as I made my way to the bathroom to try to tidy myself up before going out.

I knew I should be in bed—I had a bandage on my forehead and a headache that felt more like an earthquake. But Benji had been gone far longer than I had anticipated—the sheriff had dropped us off at the hotel hours ago. The only conclusion I could come to was that either Benji was in trouble or he was investigating the outlaw's death.

I didn't like either of the options, but if it had to be one of them, I really hoped it was the latter.

7

The moment I stepped out of the saloon and onto the walkway, my head erupted in pain, and I squeezed my eyes shut. Either someone had turned up the sun to death-ray mode, or light sensitivity was another thing I was going to have to deal with over the next few days.

I pulled in a deep breath, knowing I shouldn't be out here. But Benji needed me. I could feel it.

I slowly opened my eyes until I could just make out the walkway in front of me, and with eyes half shut, I began the not-so-far journey to the sheriff's station. I'd just taken my pain medication, and within thirty minutes, I'd be fine. Fingers crossed.

It took twice as long to get there than it should have, and when I walked through the front door of the station, I released a long sigh of relief, relishing the dim interior light.

"Are you okay?" a man asked. I glanced up to see the deputy from the evening before, his eyebrow raised. He rested his arms on the counter in front of him and gave me a look of concern.

I smiled, even though I felt like crying. "Never been better. I believe my husband is meeting with the sheriff. Mind if I head back and join them," I looked at the deputy's name tag, having already forgotten his name, "Steve?"

The deputy studied me for a long moment, like he was trying to determine if I really was as okay as I professed to be. "He left with Sheriff McKnight a while ago," he finally said. "Are you sure you should be here, though? I heard what happened to you this morning, and the sheriff said you were going to be out of commission for a few days. Honestly, I'm shocked that you're doing as well as you are."

I frowned, wondering what had happened to doctor-patient confidentiality. And then the deputy gave a pointed look at my forehead, and I remembered the bandage. I supposed I did look pretty roughed up. "I'm not going to let a little thing like a desk to the head put me out of commission. Where did Benji and the sheriff go?"

The deputy didn't look like he wanted to tell me, but after being on the receiving end of my 'mom glare,' he relented. "Went back over to where you two thought you saw the body. The sheriff and your husband had already combed the area earlier, but I guess he felt they may have missed something."

I didn't miss the emphasis on the fact that Benji and I had *thought* we saw a body. The deputy didn't believe we actually had, and it made me wonder if the sheriff was only humoring Benji.

"Thank you. I'll go see if they need any help. Because we did see a body. It wasn't our imagination. And we're going to help you find it."

Deputy Steve hesitated, like there was something he felt he should tell me but he was unsure how to say it.

"I know you don't believe me," I said, making it easier for him. "But we're not crazy."

The deputy shook his head, his voice softening. "It's not that. I know you think you saw our outlaw, and maybe you did see someone, but it wasn't Jeremy."

"He's missing, isn't he?"

Steve nodded slowly. "Yes. And so is fifty thousand dollars from our local bank. That robbery yesterday afternoon was real. During the show, Jeremy somehow took off with not only the prepared bag that was filled with random items to give shape and weight to it, but also a couple of bags that were filled with valuables stolen from several safety deposit boxes. And he never returned. He's long gone, as is his horse. If you saw a body last night, it was either a fake or someone else. Either way, you've been set up. We all have been."

I suddenly felt faint, and I had to grab onto the counter

to keep myself upright. The outlaw had stolen items worth fifty thousand dollars and fled town—so whose body had Benji and I discovered?

"Does Sheriff McKnight believe we saw a body last night?"

The deputy raised a shoulder, looking uncomfortable. "No one else in town has been reported missing."

That was a no.

"Why is Sheriff McKnight humoring my husband, combing the woods like that, if she believes that Jeremy is long gone?"

Steve's gaze dropped. "Because, as much as she wants to believe Jeremy robbed the bank and left town, she has to make certain that you two didn't see what you say you did. Jeremy is Tess's—sorry, Sheriff McKnight's—brother. She'd rather him be a thief than be dead."

I couldn't hide my surprise at the admission.

"How horrible," I said. "This has to be such a difficult time for her. Is she really the one who should be investigating her brother's disappearance?"

"Maybe that's what we need," Deputy Steve said. "Someone who is fueled by emotion. She's the best sheriff this town has ever had, and if something has happened to Jeremy—if he is dead and hasn't run off like everyone is saying—Tess won't stop until she gets justice."

"Is she looking for justice, or revenge?" I asked, afraid I already knew the answer.

Deputy Steve shrugged. "Is there a difference?" He

seemed to truly believe it was merely a matter of semantics.

"There's a really big difference."

Steve gave me a half-smile, like he found the idea amusing. I worried that there would be others in town with the same attitude, and silly things like 'evidence' no longer mattered.

"Seems like you have a tight-knit town who really cares about each other," I said. "Does the sheriff have other family that live in town?"

Steve confirmed my fear and nodded. "The McKnights were one of the founding families of our town. You throw a rock, and you'll hit at least three of them. Dusty Ridge is a dying town, and we're trying to keep it alive, but finding folks who will agree to move here...well... There aren't many who are willing to give up everything to come and run a Wild West show. Even fewer agree to raise their families here. Without the McKnights, we wouldn't stand a chance."

In Dusty Ridge's power dynamic, Sheriff McKnight already had law enforcement and healthcare professional covered—I wondered what other positions of power the family held.

All of them, I was assuming.

And that had the potential to be very dangerous.

"I appreciate your time, Steve," I said, stepping away from the counter. "I better catch up with Benji and the sheriff to see if they've found anything."

Deputy Steve suddenly looked nervous, like maybe he was just realizing he might have overshared. "Happy to help," he said. "But take my advice, you should head back to the hotel. No offense, but you're not looking so great."

I would have been offended by the comment if I believed it was true.

However, my pain medication was starting to work, and I wasn't feeling so bad now.

"Thanks. I'll consider it," I said, and then gave him a quick wave of farewell before stepping back out into the sun. I braced myself for the sharp pain but was instead met with a dull headache. Thank goodness it was nothing compared to what it had been.

My gaze swept over the street, and I tried to imagine what it would be like to live here as a child. If you were a McKnight, it was likely a wonderful life. Your childhood would be filled with the excitement that came with living in a tourist town and meeting people from all walks of life. You had the mountains that towered over you, along with trees as far as the eye could see.

It was idyllic.

Or so it would seem.

An argument caught my attention, and I glanced across the street to a man and woman having a heated exchange. Judging by the age difference, it seemed they might be grandfather and granddaughter. At first, I thought they might be tourists, until the older man glanced my way and I realized that I recognized both of them. The man had been the one in the museum that morning who'd noticed that the noose was missing, and the woman was Amy, our receptionist from the saloon. She looked a lot different without her red sequined dress. Normal.

The gentleman's gaze met mine, and he instantly recognized me.

"You," he said, leaving Amy still fuming, and he beelined across the street toward me. "You're the woman who was injured this morning."

I gently touched the bandage on my forehead, realizing it was like placing a neon sign above my head and asking people to stare. "Yes. I'm Maddie. I'm sorry we didn't have the chance to speak more this morning."

The man stuck out a hand. "I'm Seth Bloomfield, and I own the saloon that you and your husband are staying in."

Bloomfield. "Amy must be your..." I couldn't decide on daughter or granddaughter.

He smiled. "Amy is my youngest daughter, and she speaks very highly of you both. I'm just sorry that you got caught up in all of that this morning. And for Chuck to throw you into the desk like that... I know you won't believe me when I tell you that wasn't like Chuck at all. He's the least violent person you'll ever meet." He paused. "Tess told me you didn't want him arrested—that show's true character, you know, having compassion for those who hurt us."

"Emotions had been running high, and it's human

nature to react strongly to a perceived threat," I said, shrugging off the compliment. "It's how we survive."

Seth chuckled. "You sound like a shrink."

From the way he said it, it wasn't a compliment.

"That's because I am one—or at least, a psychologist."

Seth parted his lips, unsure how to recover gracefully from his mistake.

"You'll have to forgive Dad," Amy said, walking up. "My mom made him go to couples counseling, and he swears that their therapist is the reason they got a divorce. He's been a bit salty toward the profession ever since."

"I don't blame you one bit," I said. "There are good psychologists out there, and there are terrible ones. I'm sorry you had to go through that."

Amy smiled. "This was years ago, and truth be told, she was a wonderful therapist and their divorce had nothing to do with their counseling sessions. Sadly, their therapist moved on to bigger and better things outside of Dusty Ridge, and there's been no one to replace her. I don't suppose you're looking for a job, are you?"

"We don't need no damn shrink," Seth muttered to his daughter. He glanced at me. "No offense."

"Well, maybe if we had had one, then Jeremy wouldn't have—" Amy's words cut off at the fire that flashed in Seth's eyes. I had a feeling that this had been the source of their argument.

"Jeremy McKnight," I said, my voice soft. "The outlaw."

Amy hesitated but then nodded. "Yes. I'm told that you

and your husband claim to have discovered his body last night in the woods but that it had been removed by the time Tess arrived."

I stifled a groan. Dusty Ridge was the perfect place to get away with murder. Anything the sheriff learned, the rest of the town would know ten minutes later. Not hard to stay ahead of law enforcement if you knew what they did.

"That's true," I said.

Amy's gaze met mine, and it didn't waver. "You must have been mistaken. Jeremy left town—we all saw him. Robbed the bank and never looked back." Her gaze dropped. "Not even to—"

"Apologize," Seth said, cutting his daughter off. "He owed you that much for all he's put you through."

Amy stiffened, and I could feel the rage that suddenly sprang up—it radiated off her, but she remained silent.

"Can you tell me more about Jeremy?" I asked, attempting nonchalance, like it was idle curiosity that had led me to ask the question. Like I hadn't noticed that he had meant something to Amy—that they'd meant something to each other.

"There's only one thing you need to know," Seth said. "Whether Jeremy was wearing his costume or he wasn't, it didn't matter. He was the same person either way. An outlaw."

"Got into trouble often, I suppose," I said.

Seth nodded. "Even though Jeremy and Tess are siblings, they couldn't be more different if they'd tried.

Sometimes I think she went into law enforcement to try to protect him—keep him in line. Not that it did any good."

"That's unfair, Dad," Amy protested. "Jeremy... He's complicated."

Her dad shook his head. "He is not complicated. He is terrible for you, and he is terrible for this town. Your feelings have clouded your judgment."

"He's a kind man, and he loves his family."

"Except when he's drunk or out of money or looking for a tourist who can show him a good time. Did you forget about all the nights you've asked if you could stay at my house? Just until he slept it off or calmed down or—"

Amy's eyes narrowed in anger. "Fine. Yes. Jeremy isn't perfect. But he was trying. Tess saw it. I saw it. That's all he needed—someone to believe in him."

"You give him more credit than he deserves. And he knew it," Seth said. "That's why he left. Couldn't live with the guilt."

Amy's entire body tightened. "I have to get back to the saloon." She glanced at me. "Maddison, should I have dinner prepared for you and Benji tonight, or do you think you'll be out on the town?"

"I think we'll eat in tonight, thank you," I said, attempting a smile. The tension between the father and daughter, however, was suffocating, and I was having a hard time of it.

As Amy turned to walk away, I said, "I didn't know Jeremy. But I do remember those eyes. He passed our car as he raced out of town. Even beneath that mask, his joy was unmistakable. I don't think he was planning on leaving you—or this town."

Amy glanced back and gave me a sad smile. "Unfortunately, you're probably wrong. He was always happiest when he was running away."

Seth watched his daughter as she crossed the street and disappeared inside the saloon. "I don't mean to make her upset," he said with a sigh. "I just hated watching her waste her life on that McKnight boy. He wasn't good for her, and everyone knew it, except her. Even Tess tried warning Amy." His voice hitched. "My Amy deserves so much more."

"Do you think Amy might have known it more than people realized?" I asked, musing out loud. It wasn't until Seth's gaze snapped up that I realized it had been a thought I should have kept to myself.

"You're saying she wanted out of the relationship and didn't know how." He was quiet, pondering the thought. "You're suggesting she told him to leave? And now that he actually did it, she's feeling guilty about sending him away."

Seth was still operating under the assumption that Jeremy had left town with the valuables—no one here wanted to believe that he might be dead.

Because that meant that one of them might have killed him.

"I don't know anything right now," I said. "Sheriff

McKnight dropped me off at home after the altercation this morning, and I haven't spoken to her since."

What I did know was that Amy had been in an abusive relationship, and if the McKnights were as powerful as I suspected they were, they would do anything to protect each other.

For Amy, there may have only been one way out.

8

I immediately regretted the thought—I didn't want to believe it was in Amy's nature to kill someone. From our limited interactions, she seemed like a kind and decent person.

Not only that, she wasn't strong enough to hoist a man into the air with nothing but a rope. If she had been involved in Jeremy's death, she would have needed help.

"I wasn't suggesting that Jeremy's disappearance is Amy's fault," I told Seth.

He studied me. "You think I was involved, then. I know I wasn't a fan of the guy, but—" His words cut off, his gaze landing over my shoulder.

I turned to follow his gaze and saw the sheriff's squad car pull around the corner and drive toward us.

Seth glanced down the street. "You think she found something?"

"I don't know," I said as the car slowed. "Maybe."

But it wasn't Sheriff McKnight who jumped out of the car when it came to a stop next to us—she stayed in the driver's seat. It was Benji. And he did not look happy with me.

"What are you doing outside?" he asked, rushing to my side.

"I needed some fresh air," I said. "Besides, Seth was keeping an eye on me."

Benji glanced at Seth, who gave him a nod hello.

"Speaking of, I better get back to check on Amy," Seth said, resting a hand on my shoulder. "You let us know if you need anything." And then the older man crossed the street, casting anxious glances at the sheriff's car as he went.

Benji took my hands in his and looked me in the eyes, as if he could tell if something was wrong by staring hard enough. "This morning you crashed into a desk and were momentarily unconscious."

"Yes, I remember. Or at least, I remember some of it," I said, smiling. It wasn't at all funny, but I hoped it might help Benji lighten up a little. I could not be trapped in that hotel room for the rest of our honeymoon, no matter how nice it was.

"Tell her the part about the importance of rest and hydration," Sheriff McKnight called through the open car window.

Benji's lips twitched up as he recited the message back

to me. "I've heard that rest and hydration are really important after a traumatic event, such as a concussion."

"And I've heard that it's important for a husband and
wife to be together on their honeymoon," I said, lowering
my voice so only Benji could hear. "And for that husband
to not leave her alone if he inserts himself into a murder
investigation."

Benji raised his shoulders in a helpless shrug. "You
needed the rest, and Sheriff McKnight needed to know
where we saw the body."

"You find anything?" I asked.

"Nothing."

That was disappointing, though not surprising. "The
killer likely returned early this morning to get rid of any
evidence." I glanced over at the squad car, where Sheriff
McKnight had her phone up to her ear, but I doubted
anyone was on the other end of that call, considering how
often her gaze was jumping to us. "The locals still think
Jeremy robbed the bank and left town."

"As frustrating as it is, it makes sense," Benji said.
"There's no body, so we can't prove Jeremy is dead."

Just because it made sense didn't mean I had to
like it.

"How hard was Sheriff McKnight actually looking for
that evidence today?" I asked.

Benji hesitated. "I didn't doubt her intentions, if that's
what you're asking."

"Good intentions aren't enough. If she believes Jeremy

ran off with those valuables, it doesn't matter what we say. Someone is going to get away with murder."

"We told Sheriff McKnight about the dead outlaw before he was ever reported as missing," Benji said. "Surely that has to count for something—it's too much to be a coincidence."

I glanced over to where the sheriff was still waiting in her car, watching us. "Let's go get some dinner, shall we?" I said loudly. "I think you are right—I need to rest."

Benji looked at me like I'd lost my mind but then noticed my gaze flicker over to the sheriff's car, and his expression opened in understanding. "Oh. Right. I'm so glad to hear you say that. Rest is exactly what you need." He turned toward the squad car and gave the sheriff a little wave. "I'm sorry I couldn't be more help," he called.

"You helped plenty," she called back. And then she drove the last block and parked in front of the sheriff's station.

Benji took my hand, and I had never been more grateful for someone to lean on. "Do you actually want to have dinner, or was that something you said just to get rid of the sheriff?"

"I always want dinner, whether I'm using it as an excuse or not. Food is my love language."

Benji laughed and pulled me in for a kiss. "Very true. It was a silly question."

"Amy is making dinner for us at the saloon," I said, leading him across the street. "But I do need to talk to you about some things I learned. Like the fact that the missing outlaw, Jeremy, is Sheriff McKnight's brother. Did she happen to mention that little fact while you two were out sleuthing?"

From Benji's slack expression, she hadn't. "That's kind of an important detail," he muttered. "And given the situation, I'm surprised she hasn't been taking our claims more seriously."

"Maybe that's the point," I said. "She doesn't want our help. She might believe us—she might suspect foul play. But as far as she's concerned, we're two random tourists who claim to have discovered the body of her brother—a body that is no longer where we said we'd found it. That makes us unreliable witnesses."

Music erupted from my pocket, and I held up a finger, indicating that this conversation was not yet over.

Lilly.

Of all my family, I'd thought she'd be the one most likely to give Benji and me the space we needed for our honeymoon.

"Hey, hon. Everything all right?" I asked, answering the call.

"With us? Yeah, everything's fine," Lilly said. "But what about with you two? I know you said that the sheriff's station is a popular tourist attraction there, but you two seem to be spending an awful lot of time there for being on your honeymoon."

I glanced across the street at the sheriff's station.

Sheriff McKnight had already gone inside, her squad car sitting empty. "Honestly, Lilly, you two need to stop tracking my phone. This is absolutely an invasion of privacy and—"

"Answer the question, Mom. Are you two okay?"

"Yes, we're fine. Right now, we're standing across the street from the sheriff's office. We're not even inside. I'd get a more accurate tracking app if I were you."

"But you and Benji were there last night. And Benji was there earlier today, right?"

I released a frustrated sigh. "Yes, he was, because of the accident at the museum. I've already told you this."

"Why was Benji at the sheriff's office, if you're the one who was injured?" she retorted.

This was my fault. My children had acquired their inquisitive natures from me, and I'd encouraged them by allowing them to be a part of investigations in the past. It wasn't like there was an off switch where I could just make them stop.

I glanced at Benji, unsure what to do.

He merely shrugged, like he was telling me, *I think you know there is only one way this is going to end.*

"Lilly, honestly, Benji and I are on our way to dinner. Can we catch up when we return at the end of the week? Please?"

"Fine. Just one more question."

I rubbed my forehead. My headache was returning

with a vengeance, and I was feeling unsteady on my feet. I grabbed onto Benji's arm to help stabilize myself.

"If it's quick."

"Are you investigating?"

I didn't want to lie to my daughter, and I was unsure how to answer that. My vision was swimming, and I'd be lucky to make it back to my and Benji's room, let alone find a missing person. I supposed that meant that no, we weren't.

"No, Lilly. We're just trying to have dinner."

"Then why is there a missing person report with the Colorado police? And when we dig deeper into the police report, you and Benji are listed as potential witnesses."

9

My headache was coming on stronger.

"Are you two so bored that the only thing you can think of doing is tracking your mom, and breaking a few laws while doing it?" I said, my tone harsher than I had intended. I sucked in a deep breath. "Lilly, it was one thing to snoop when we were involved in an investigation back home, but you can't pry into people's lives just because you feel like it."

"We didn't do it because we felt like it, we did it because we were concerned," Lilly protested. "There's a difference."

"Well, we're not investigating anyone's disappearance, so you can stop worrying," I said.

I pulled on Benji's arm, letting him know that I needed to stop walking for a moment. I eased myself onto a bench in front of the barbershop and rested my head against the window.

"You promise?" Lilly asked.

"Yes. Now, my head is killing me and I need some food. Please don't track me anymore, and I'll see you two at the end of the week."

"Okay. Sorry," Lilly said, her voice small. "We just thought that if you were looking for the guy, we could help. I guess that means you won't need the information we dug up on Jeremy McKnight or his family's feud with the Bloomfields."

I sat up straighter. "Sorry, there's a feud?"

Other than Seth Bloomfield's disapproval of Jeremy dating his daughter, I hadn't noticed any animosity between folks in town. If anything, they were overprotective.

Unless they were only overprotective of their own families. It made me wonder if the groundskeeper, Chuck, was related to Peggy, the woman at the museum. Maybe that was why he'd jumped into superhero mode. That would explain her argument with Seth, considering he was a Bloomfield.

"It's none of our business, and we don't want to pry into others' personal lives," Lilly said, echoing my words. "I hope you feel better, though. Getting hurt is not a fun way to start your honeymoon. And I promise, we won't track your location anymore. Love you."

Before she could hang up, I said, "Lilly, wait." I knew

this wasn't a proud parenting moment, rewarding my kids for what they obviously shouldn't have been doing. But I needed to know more about this feud. "Will you send me whatever research you have? Just to be safe."

Lilly saw through me, even over the phone, and I could hear her smiling, her voice suddenly far too chipper as she said, "Oh, yeah, no problem. Anything to help keep you safe. Who knew that Dusty Ridge would be such a war zone?"

I'd have bet anything that she'd only pretended she was about to hang up, knowing I'd stop her.

I didn't know if I should be impressed or frightened at the children I'd raised.

"Our honeymoon has certainly turned out to be more interesting than I had anticipated," I told her.

"We'll send over our findings in the next few minutes. Love you."

The line went quiet, and I saw she'd hung up.

"What was that about?" Benji asked, his expression concerned. "Your kids aren't pulling you into something, are they?"

Benji loved my kids, but he knew how impulsive they could be—and how they'd gotten that from their mother.

"That depends on how you look at it," I said. "Let's just say that my kids need to move away and start their new jobs. This in-between time isn't good for them—they're bored."

Benji waited for me to continue, knowing there was more. "And?" he prompted.

"And the natural result was them tracking my movements over the last twenty-four hours, noticing how often we go to the sheriff's station and then trying to figure out why." I tried to make it sound normal, like something that everyone's teenagers did.

"And did they?" Benji asked, though I could tell he already knew the answer.

I hesitated but then nodded. "It looks like Sheriff McKnight really doesn't believe us about finding a body— or maybe she's holding onto hope that her brother is still out there somewhere, alive. She filed a missing person report with the state, and we are listed as potential witnesses. Which, of course, led the kids to dig deeper."

I had Benji's full attention now. "And?"

"And..." I glanced around us. This wasn't a safe place to talk about the things Lilly had told me. I nodded toward the saloon. "How do you feel about room service?"

Benji stood, extending a hand to me. "Sounds perfect. I've had enough running around for one day."

When we entered the saloon, neither Seth nor Amy was around. We did hear yelling from the back, though. It sounded like they hadn't finished the conversation they'd started out on the street.

"We'll let them calm down first," Benji said, looking like he wanted nothing to do with their domestic squabble.

I agreed and followed him onto the elevator.

We stayed silent until we stepped into our suite—once we were sure no one would be able to hear us.

"So, what didn't you want to talk about out there?" Benji asked, helping me to the sofa.

"Flash did some research, and it turns out there is quite the feud going on between the Bloomfields and the McKnights. Lilly is supposed to be emailing me what they found—mind grabbing my laptop for me?"

Benji stilled, his mind having gone elsewhere.

"My laptop?" I said again.

He shook himself from it. "Yeah. Sorry." Benji grabbed it from the night table and brought it to me. "You're saying that the Bloomfield family could have killed Jeremy because of this rivalry?"

"Maybe. I want to read through this research before I start making any assumptions."

"That would explain why the sheriff is brushing us off," Benji mumbled as I looked through my email.

I glanced up. "You think that even if she believed us, she would never admit it."

He nodded. "If people think Jeremy was murdered, and this feud is as bad as you make it sound, this town could turn into a real-life Western shootout."

That seemed a bit dramatic, especially coming from someone like Benji. Until I opened the email.

"Listen to this," I said, leaning forward to better read the small print. "The two men who founded this town were Ewan McKnight and Jacob Bloomfield. They were best friends who came out West shortly before the gold rush. When they hit it big, they brought their families out here—parents, grandparents, cousins...everyone."

"Enough people to start a town," Benji said.

"Yeah. Some other folks came out here with them— friends of friends, that kind of thing. But it was the McKnights and Bloomfields who ran the town."

Benji flopped onto the couch beside me and cozied up. I smiled and intertwined my hand with his before turning back to the computer.

"So, when did this feud start?" he asked.

I scanned the article. "Doesn't say." I closed it and opened up the next one. After a quick scan, I found new information in the last paragraph. "It looks like Jacob Bloomfield was appointed sheriff—he'd been a deputy when they'd lived back East and was a natural choice. Ewan McKnight was manager of the town."

"So, he was essentially the mayor."

I nodded. "Yeah. But they had some disagreements on how it should be run, and Ewan basically told Jacob that he was in charge of managing the town, and they were going to do it how he wanted. It seems that there was some favoritism toward his own family, and he was okay bending the laws and making concessions where they were concerned."

"But I bet he wasn't bending the rules for the Bloom-fields," Benji guessed.

"Right again. The argument got so heated that Ewan

McKnight essentially fired Jacob and made his own brother sheriff. Now two McKnight men were in the most powerful positions in town."

Benji leaned back, crossing his arms. "And there is still a McKnight as sheriff today. I'm assuming the same goes for their mayor."

"Probably." I skimmed through another couple of articles that basically said the same thing. Over the years, the McKnights had slowly siphoned power away from the Bloomfields, leaving them with very little. It had gotten so bad that most of the Bloomfields had left town. As much as the McKnights had grown to dislike the Bloomfields, they'd needed them. There weren't enough of the McKnight family to run the entire town, especially because many of their own family were choosing to move away and live their lives elsewhere.

I leaned back and nestled under Benji's arm. "So, two best friends move out West and become rich. Enough so that they bring their families and friends out here to join them. But one favors his family over the other. Slowly, over time, that imbalance of power creates enough animosity that the less powerful family starts to leave. The ones that stay choose to fight back. In these articles, there are stories of buildings burning down without cause and that kind of thing, but I can't see any record of murders. Why start now?"

Benji was quiet as he played with my hair.

"What if there were, but they were recorded as accidents?" he finally said. "If your family is both the sheriff and the mayor, it wouldn't be difficult to make those things disappear. Much like Jeremy."

"But Jeremy was a McKnight," I said. "They aren't going to kill their own family members."

He gave me a side glance. "And yet, no one knows where Jeremy is."

10

I was so absorbed in the articles I was rereading that I didn't hear the elevator approach when Seth brought up our dinner. He knocked on the privacy door, announcing his presence, and I jumped halfway off the sofa, startled by the interruption. Benji shot me an amused look as he walked to the door, and I slammed my laptop shut, not wanting Seth to catch a glimpse of what I was reading.

"Chicken fried steak with mashed potatoes and gravy, grilled vegetables, and a brownie for dessert," Seth announced as he carried two trays to the coffee table in front of me. He looked for a place to set them down.

In my hurry to close the laptop, I'd forgotten about all the notes I'd been taking, trying to keep my thoughts organized. I quickly gathered up the notepads, allowing Seth to set down the food, but not before he saw what was written on them.

The older gentleman looked between Benji and me, not in anger or annoyance but with curiosity.

"Why are two young people on their honeymoon studying the history of an old tourist town?" he asked. "You two should be taking pictures on the movie sets, or going on a tour up to the ghost towns. Instead, you're sitting around, taking notes on old rivalries that don't even exist anymore."

I tilted my head to the side. "Don't exist. You mean, there's no longer animosity between the Bloomfields and the McKnights?"

Seth's eyebrows knit in suspicion. "Are you actually honeymooners? Seems you're more like documentarians." A pause. "Is that a word? Documentarians?"

I honestly had no idea, but it sounded good to me. Except Seth had gotten the wrong idea about us, and if he thought we were undercover journalists, it wouldn't be long until the whole town thought it.

"We actually are on our honeymoon," I said, my voice firm. I'd meant to sound resolute—like he could trust us. Instead, it sounded like I was trying to cover up something —like I was overcompensating for a lie. "But, as you know, I'm a psychologist," I said, softening my tone. "And I find your town fascinating—a place that is untouched by time, where people stay for generations, never leaving."

That should placate him.

Seth gave a satisfied nod. "I was right. You're here to study our town. Documentarians."

"That's not at all what I was saying," I started, but Seth wasn't listening. He'd already made up his mind.

I threw a pleading glance at Benji, and he stepped in.

"We aren't journalists," he said. "I chose the location of our honeymoon, and, honestly, Maddie wasn't convinced she'd like it until we drove into town and we were enveloped in the authenticity of it all. It sent us down a rabbit hole, researching the beginnings of the town, which movies were filmed here—you really do live in a fascinating place."

Seth folded his arms over his chest. "Documentarians."

Nothing we said would explain the notes he had seen on the table, and nothing would convince him that we were indeed on our honeymoon and we hadn't come under false pretenses in order to research their town. If Seth told everyone that we were there to spy on them, they'd all clam up and we'd never discover what had happened to Jeremy.

"We're trying to find Jeremy McKnight," I blurted out. As soon as I said it, I knew it had been a mistake. That chicken fried steak smelled amazing, and it was going to be cold by the time Seth was done with us. He didn't believe anything we said anyway, so it wasn't like it mattered.

Except he did believe me.

Both Benji and Seth stilled.

"Why would you care about finding a random guy you've never met?" Seth asked.

I met his gaze. "We saw him hanging from a noose in the woods, and no one will believe us."

Seth raised an eyebrow. "That's because Jeremy skipped town on that horse of his after robbing the bank. I'm sure you've heard by now, with all that research, that items valued at nearly fifty thousand dollars have been missing since Jeremy disappeared. He could be anywhere —what you're searching for is a ghost."

I frowned. "What we saw was very real. Someone killed Jeremy, and that same person likely has those valuables that you claim are missing."

"They'd have a hard time hiding that kind of loot," Seth said. "If you hadn't noticed, folks around here don't have a lot."

"True, but it's a lot easier if you have help. And someone to share the money with."

Seth's eyes narrowed. "You think a member of my family did it—you think it was a Bloomfield. That's why you were asking about the feud."

I tried to deny it, but I couldn't. When I opened my mouth but no sound came out, Seth released a long sigh and shook his head.

"The Bloomfields and McKnights have had our prob-lems," he said. "But we mended that rift decades ago—back when I was a kid. Even if we hadn't, we wouldn't take an innocent life. We're not that kind of people."

"What if someone didn't consider Jeremy innocent," I asked. "You certainly don't."

Benji nudged me and shook his head. He wanted me to back off.

I realized I was probably taking things too far—Seth was going to think I was accusing him of something. Honestly, I hadn't ruled him out. Someone in this town had killed Jeremy, and they had expertly covered it up. As far as I knew, it could easily have been a family project— the Bloomfields sending a message.

We had no proof that Seth had been a part of it, though. And the look on his face right now—it didn't just hold anger. There was also fear.

"What you saw earlier between Amy and me—it was nothing more than a father's concern for his daughter."

"There was a lot of emotion behind that concern," I said.

Seth's entire body tensed. "Of course there was," he snapped. "If you'd seen the things I have, you'd be emotional too. My daughter has been hurt, both physically and emotionally, by a man she trusted—a man she grew up with—and I want nothing more than to protect her. I feel powerless because she won't let me." Seth's voice was rising, and despair laced each word. "So, yes. This leaves me emotional. I no longer have a family or a town that values me or my opinions. So, forgive me if I don't care much about Jeremy disappearing into the night. I say good riddance. That is one less person I need to worry about. He could have taken the whole town with him, and I wouldn't care."

I took a tentative step forward. "Yes, you would," I said. "Because as frustrated you are with this town and as angry as you are with everyone in it, you still care about them. Like you said, Jeremy and Amy grew up together. They probably rode their bikes on these walkways while you called out for them to be careful. You were probably friends with his parents and got together to grill burgers and set off fireworks on the Fourth of July. These people were your friends. But something has changed." I paused. "Has there been a renewed conflict between the Bloom-fields and the McKnights?"

Seth stared at me. "You really are a psychologist, huh?"

My lips twitched up at the corners. "Yup. And this morning I noticed your frustration at not being docent at the museum, even though you know this town better than anyone. Why isn't it you who was given the position there?"

Seth released a sigh. "Back when I was young, the Bloomfields and McKnights had started to mend the rift that Ewan and Jacob had set in motion. By the time my wife and I had Amy, there was no 'us versus them.' But, gradually, people started reverting to the old ways. At first it was just a cranky old timer or two, but their attitude caught. Especially among those it benefited."

"The McKnight family," I guessed.

He hesitated. "I don't like to point fingers."

Interesting comment. If it was the McKnights, and there were hard feelings toward the family, why wouldn't he call them out? Did that mean he truly didn't wish ill on the family? Or was it that it wasn't the McKnights who had reopened the rift at all—it had been the Bloomfields?

11

B y the time Benji and I got to our chicken fried steak, it was cold, but that was our fault. We'd been the ones to keep Seth talking—or, more correctly, I had been.

My mind drifted as I used my fork to scoop some mashed potatoes onto the chicken.

Before Seth had brought up our dinner, I'd suspected he might be our killer—saving his daughter from the abusive man she couldn't bring herself to leave. But Seth wasn't a murderer. He was a sad man who felt like he'd been tossed aside—forgotten. There weren't many Bloomfields left, but I imagined they might feel the same way as Seth.

Lonely.

Of course, it was often those who had been brushed aside who were the most dangerous—they had nothing left to lose.

My head had begun throbbing again, and I reached across the table for the pain medication.

"You're awfully quiet," I said, watching Benji as he worked on his own dinner. "Everything okay?"

Benji nodded slowly, but it morphed into a shake of the head. "I wish we could rewind time to this morning. When we went over to the museum, we'd convinced ourselves that we'd seen a ghost—or at least a fake body. I was so sure that someone had pranked us. But since then, you've been attacked and injured, and we've somehow gotten ourselves involved in an investigation that we shouldn't be anywhere near. There is no body. No one is asking for our help." He turned his sad brown puppy-dog eyes on me. "We have no business chasing a bank robber, and we've done our civic duty by answering all of the sheriff's questions and showing her where we saw the body."

His words made me pause. And guilt pricked at me.

Benji was right. Here I was, steamrolling ahead as usual, when I had no need to. We were on our honeymoon. If the town wasn't worried about Jeremy's disappearance, why should we be? Benji needed me more than Sheriff McKnight did.

"You're right," I said, leaning forward and kissing him. "Tonight, we relax here. Tomorrow morning, we go out on an adventure. And I don't mean the investigate murders type of adventure. One that is just for us."

Benji's forehead crinkled in amusement. "Or we take it

easy and enjoy our Saloon Suite. You aren't supposed to be pushing it too hard, you know. Doctor's orders."

"Exercise is good for a person, and surely she wouldn't object to a nice morning walk."

He laughed, obviously relieved that he'd moved me off the subject of disappearing outlaws and back onto what was important.

Us.

So, that was what I was going to focus on. And I would push down the nagging thought in the back of my mind that we were missing something—something important that could prove that Jeremy had been murdered.

Because that was someone else's problem.

I kissed Benji again to prove it.

THE SUN ROSE FAR TOO EARLY, and I rolled over, using my pillow to try to hide from it.

But then I smelled the sweet scent of syrup. I poked my head out to see a plate of French toast coated with powdered sugar and strawberries. A small bottle of syrup sat on the breakfast tray next to it, along with a glass of orange juice.

"Is that a hundred percent syrup?" I asked, poking my head out further.

"The purest," Benji said with a smile. "Straight from Canada."

Oh, it smelled so good.

I pushed myself into a sitting position, expecting my head to explode with the movement. Only it didn't.

"Hey, I'm feeling a lot better," I said. "Must be all the fresh air and good food from yesterday."

Benji's smile momentarily dipped, but he recovered so fast, it seemed he'd hoped I hadn't noticed.

"What's wrong?" I asked as he slid the tray onto my lap.

Benji took a moment to make sure I was settled before he said, "I'm happy you're feeling better—that's a lot faster than normal for a concussion."

I shrugged. "I got a good night's sleep last night."

"True," Benji said slowly. "But we don't know that you had a concussion, right? A laceration, yes. A terrible headache, of course. But how do we know you had a concussion?"

"Probably because I hit my head with enough force to knock me momentarily unconscious, and blunt force trauma tends to give a person a concussion."

Benji nodded. "Yes, but no one did any imaging. You haven't felt nauseous or confused, or some of the other more common side effects."

"I have been sensitive to light."

"But that's pretty typical when you have a headache."

I studied Benji as I sipped my orange juice. This type of questioning—it was the kind of thing I would do. Not Benji.

"What are you getting at?"

Benji hesitated for a second before plunging ahead.

"What if Sheriff McKnight told you that you had a concussion and needed to rest for the next few days because she wanted us out of the way? Because she knew we would find things that she wanted to remain hidden?"

This was definitely not like Benji. And it was concerning.

"What happened to us forgetting about all that and enjoying our honeymoon?" I asked. "We're going out on an adventure today, remember? Enjoying each other's company. Not investigating bank robbers."

Benji nodded. "I'm very aware. But last night, every time I closed my eyes, I saw Jeremy. Staring. Lifeless." He pulled in a shuddered breath. "That wasn't a prank, Maddie. And that person thinks they've gotten away with murder."

Now that I looked at Benji more closely, I could see that his eyes were red and bloodshot. The bags under his eyes were dark, and I saw my amazing breakfast for what it was. An apology. A way to soften the blow that we needed to continue investigating Jeremy's disappearance. That this wasn't the honeymoon we'd hoped it would be.

"You want to investigate," I said slowly. It was taking me a minute to wrap my head around what Benji was saying—this wasn't our usual dynamic.

He nodded. "It's not so much that I want to, but I feel that we need to."

Benji had officially crossed over to the dark side—this

was what I felt on a daily basis. And once you crossed over, you could never go back.

"You do understand what you're suggesting, don't you?" I said. "We'd be getting involved in an investigation that this town wants to keep quiet. We don't know anyone here, and we can't turn to anyone for help. Seth and Amy are just as likely to be involved as Sheriff McKnight and her deputy. There's the lady who runs the museum and Chuck and whoever is in that weird place with the green door that Chuck tried to lead us to. We literally can't trust anyone here."

Benji's eyes lit up. "That's where we're going to start."

Oh, dear, now he really was starting to sound like me. I wished he wouldn't.

"Did you hear a thing I just said?" I asked. "Last night you helped me realize that we shouldn't get involved in whatever this is. This feels bigger than we can handle—I don't think that just one person is involved. I wouldn't be surprised if half the town is."

Benji nodded. "Yes, I heard you. And I understand. But you saw Jeremy—you saw his face."

Like Benji, I had woken up to that face haunting me. And I had been actively trying to rid myself of that image.

"I can't make an identification off that," I said. "It could be anyone."

Benji raised a finger. "And yet, you think it was Jeremy." He paused, his voice softening. "Please. I know that this is usually your territory, and this role reversal is weird and slightly uncomfortable. I also know that Jeremy wasn't even a good guy. But that doesn't mean he deserved to die."

I hated when Benji made a good point.

"All right," I relented. "It wouldn't be a Maddie and Benji honeymoon if we didn't try to find a killer. But as soon as we find him, or her, we're finishing this honeymoon the way it was meant to be started. We're getting the spa treatment and seeing those ghost towns, and everything."

Benji smiled. "Deal."

I stabbed a strawberry with my fork and twirled it in some of the syrup on my plate. "After I finished listing everyone we absolutely can't trust, you seemed to have gotten an idea," I said. "What did you mean when you said, 'That's where we're going to start?'"

Benji grew serious. "Chuck tried sending us to some sketchy basement in town. I want to know why. It could have been a distraction because he didn't want us around the museum at the time. Maybe he knew that if we stayed, we'd find the body and he was trying to do a bit of misdirection."

"Getting us to look at what doesn't matter so we don't notice what does," I said. "Like a magician—except, he does it with shovels and trimmers."

Benji nodded. "Exactly."

"So, how does giving in to that misdirection help us find who did this?" I asked. "Shouldn't we be looking for what he didn't want us looking at?"

Benji pushed his tray away, though he hadn't eaten much. "We've already tried that. We saw the body when we shouldn't have. And we scoured the area for evidence, only to not find any. The basement might have been a distraction, but whoever is in that basement might be a clue to who is involved in all this. Why did Chuck send us there specifically? He could have sent us anywhere—even just back to our hotel."

"Sending us off to follow clues would have given Chuck more time to get rid of the body," I said. "It would ensure that we wouldn't be hanging around this area of town for a while. It doesn't mean that whoever, or whatever, is there had anything to do with Jeremy's death."

Benji stood. "True. But how about we find out?"

12

I held my phone out in front of me as if it were a compass. "Okay, we're going to turn left here, and then the hotel should be up on the right."

Benji and I stood on a street corner at a four-way intersection that had no stoplight and no stop signs.

"You're sure we don't turn right?" Benji asked, scanning the road.

"The phone doesn't lie. I took down notes exactly as Chuck said them."

"Who am I to argue with Chuck's notes?"

I laughed and pulled Benji to the left. As promised, the third building on the right was a two-story hotel with a beautiful balcony wrapped around the second floor. I could imagine all sorts of high-profile celebrities staying at it, back in the day.

But we wouldn't be going inside the hotel.

As we drew closer, the side of the building came into view, and I saw the green door that Chuck had referenced. It wasn't at street level, though. Instead, it was at the bottom of a steep staircase.

"You have a bad feeling about this?" I asked Benji, my steps slowing.

"Of course," he said. "You know how much I hate horror films—especially ones where people walk willingly into a dark basement, knowing the killer is likely down there. I have better common sense than that." Benji walked closer and stared at the door, his expression untrusting.

"The entrance to this basement is in broad daylight," I pointed out.

Benji glanced around. There weren't many people around, but there were enough to make me feel safe. "Yeah, it is," he said. "But it was getting pretty dark last night when Chuck gave us the directions."

"True."

Benji glanced around again. "What do you think?"

I hesitated. Part of me shared Benji's concerns about following random directions from a random groundskeeper and walking into an unknown basement just because he told us to. The other part? It was the side that usually won, because it housed my curiosity and my need for answers. If we didn't go in, I'd forever be wondering what we would have found.

"I think we should go in," I said. "I doubt that Chuck had something sinister planned for last night, considering we hadn't found the body yet. But even if he had planned something, we didn't come, and whoever is behind that green door won't be expecting us to show up randomly in the middle of the day. If anything, we have the element of surprise on our side."

Benji's concerned expression transitioned into a smile. "This is insane. I hope you know that."

I returned his smile. "I do."

"Good." And then he took my hand and led me down the steps. If we were going to do something crazy, we were going to do it together.

Before we even had the chance to knock, however, the green door swung open, and we were suddenly face to face with a man who was far larger than any man I'd ever met. He was tall with broad shoulders and tattoos running down both arms. He crossed his arms across his huge chest, and his steady gaze unnerved me.

"Hi," I said, my voice squeaking as I gave him a little wave. "Chuck told us we should stop by?"

It was more of a question than a statement, because I had no idea where we were or why Chuck had sent us here, but I was really hoping that both Benji and I would be walking away in one piece.

The man released a long sigh and shook his head. "Dammit, Chuck." And then his gaze returned to us and he smiled. "Well, you might as well come in." And he stepped aside, holding the door open.

I threw a questioning glance at Benji—I wasn't sure I wanted to go into the hotel's basement with a man who could kill us with one hand tied behind his back.

Benji seemed equally unsure, but the man was waiting for us to enter, and I really didn't want to annoy him, so I stepped over the threshold and into... I didn't know what I had just entered. It seemed like a metal shop or maybe a glassworks? All I knew was that directly in front of us were furnaces and tongs, thick aprons, and safety goggles.

"What is this place?" Benji asked, eyeing all the heavy equipment like it could be used on people just as easily as on metal.

The man stared at us, his expression incredulous. "Chuck didn't tell you where you were going, and you just blindly followed his directions?"

I'd known it was a crazy thing to do, but I'd thought of it as an exciting adventure.

And that was how all those people in horror movies, whom I'd always made fun of, ended up dead. They went to those dark scary basements because it was an adventure.

"To be fair," I started. And then I realized I had no excuse. "Yes, that's exactly what we did."

The man burst into laughter, and the smile he wore made him seem a lot less scary than he had a minute earlier.

He stuck out a hand. "I'm Phineas. I run this place." He glanced up at the ceiling. "Not the hotel, just the basement. Which is how I like it—this is where all the fun stuff happens."

Benji found his voice and tentatively asked, "And exactly what does happen in here? You an artist or something?"

I was surprised by the last question, but then I realized I'd missed some key details. To our right were several large metal suitcases that looked like something you'd use to protect valuable items. They had to be six feet long and three feet wide. One of the cases was open, and I could see art pieces nestled into specially designed foam. Glass cases around the room housed other art pieces, but strangely, the pieces seemed to all be exactly alike. All carbon copies of each other.

My lips parted in surprise when I realized what they were. "Benji," I whispered. "Phineas might be an artist, but that's not what he's doing here."

Phineas frowned. "Of course it's art. I do every one of those babies myself, individually. Not many people in the world have the skills that I do."

Benji's eyes widened in alarm. "He's a counterfeiter?" he whispered, though it was loud enough for Phineas to hear.

I realized my mistake in not making myself clearer, and I worried that Phineas would be offended by Benji's assumption, but instead he laughed.

"My man, these are one hundred percent real."

I squeezed Benji's arm. "You know the awards they give to musicians for best album of the year and that kind of thing? I've never actually watched the Grammys, but I know what one looks like. And we are surrounded by dozens of them."

Benji's expression was skeptical as his gaze swept the room. "You mean to tell me that the Grammys, one of the biggest award ceremonies in the world, has chosen to have their awards made in this old town, one by one, in a hotel basement?"

Phineas shrugged. "What can I tell you? Fancy people like their awards hand made, and not by some faceless factory. They want these awards to mean something." He nodded toward the open case. "I'm still working on filling up that case, but you're more than welcome to have your picture taken while holding one. Who knows, you might be holding Beyoncé's next Grammy."

"I guess you don't put their names on them before you ship them out," I said.

Phineas smiled. "Nope. Unfortunately, these go out long before anyone knows who has been nominated, let alone who won."

"Well, I, for one, would love to get my picture holding a Grammy," I said, stepping toward the open case. As I did so, my gaze fell on the glass case closest to me. My eyes widened, and I turned. "Is this Taylor Swift's broken Grammy?"

Inside the case was a Grammy that was in pieces, and someone had written *Oops!* along the side of the largest piece. I remembered images of a young girl who had won so many awards, she'd struggled to hold all of them, and she'd dropped some.

"They sent back the broken one, and I made her a new one," Phineas said, pride tinging his voice. He obviously loved what he did here. It was a good thing too, considering all the burn marks I'd noticed on his skin. It seemed it wasn't without its risks.

I turned back to the open case and reached for one of the Grammys. "You're sure this is okay?" I asked, hesitating. "What if I accidentally break it?"

"Then I'll put it in the case alongside Taylor's," he said.

Phineas gave an easy laugh, and it relaxed me. I pulled one of the awards out of the case and was surprised by the weight of it.

"You aren't kidding around with these awards," I said.

"Only the best for our musicians."

Benji picked up his own, and I handed Phineas my phone before posing for the picture. Lilly was going to be so jealous. Not that that was something to strive for, but it did give me a little thrill. Usually, I wasn't cool enough for my kids. This should change their opinion.

"Have you lived in Dusty Ridge your whole life?" I asked as I carefully placed the award back in the foam.

I wasn't just asking because I wanted to figure out why Chuck had sent us here—it could have been that he just thought we'd like to see where the Grammys were made. I honestly was interested in Phineas. He seemed like such a fascinating person.

Phineas shook his head. "I used to live in LA, actually. But I got involved in smelting and found that I longed for a slower, simpler life. I secured the contract for the Grammys before moving out here and managed to convince the owner of this hotel that I had more use for her basement than she did."

"They're lucky to have you," I said, my gaze returning to Taylor Swift's broken Grammy. "Dusty Ridge was an interesting choice. Did you choose this location so you could be closer to family?"

What I really wanted to know was if he was a Bloomfield or a McKnight. Even though Phineas was a super cool person, he was also very strong. Strong enough to be able to lift someone into a tree, for example.

Phineas didn't answer right away, and I could sense he'd put his guard up. I'd just gotten too personal.

"You're that shrink that people have been talking about," he said, stepping forward and taking Benji's Grammy from him before placing it back in the case.

I wasn't surprised that Phineas knew who we were—twenty-four hours was more than enough time for gossip to travel through town, even if we hadn't claimed we'd found a body.

"I don't love the term 'shrink,' but yes, I am a psychologist. But I wasn't asking because I wanted to psychoanalyze you, if that's what you're thinking. I just like talking to people."

Benji nodded. "It's true, she does."

Phineas gave me an amused smile. "So I've heard. I've also heard that you have some alternative theories about what happened to Jeremy McKnight."

"If by alternative theories you mean that we claimed we found a body, then that's correct. And, unless someone else was dressed up in his outlaw outfit two evenings ago, it was likely him. I haven't heard of anyone else in town being reported as missing."

Phineas closed the Grammys case, then turned to us, his expression serious. "I've also heard that you're trying to find who killed him. When talking to the sheriff didn't go how you wanted it to, you started your own research project into the history of our town."

That gave me pause.

"Seth tell you that?" Must have meant that Phineas was a Bloomfield. That definitely moved him up on my suspect list.

Phineas nodded. "He did. And he's just as concerned about Jeremy's disappearance as I am. Jeremy wasn't a great person—he wasn't even a good person. But this town has had worse than him, and no one has ever disappeared before. It means that things are escalating."

"And let me guess, you weren't involved," I said.

Phineas raised a curious eyebrow. "Why would I be involved? None of this has anything to do with me, and trust me, I don't want any trouble. Folks from the awards committee come out every once in a while to inspect my workplace and the quality of my work—make sure I'm not switching out my materials and using inferior metals, and that kind of thing. They trust me up to a certain point, but not unconditionally. And how would it look if when they come out, the McKnights are retaliating and people are showing up dead?"

Benji had been quiet for a while, studying Phineas. He rubbed his chin, his gaze never straying. "Why are you afraid the McKnights will retaliate? Everyone thinks that Jeremy robbed the bank and high-tailed it out of here. There's no need to retaliate if the Bloomfields didn't do anything wrong."

I watched Phineas's expression, expecting to see guilt at having said more than he should have.

Instead, he gave an incredulous laugh.

"No one actually thinks that Jeremy stole that stuff. Everyone just says they do so that no one truly knows what is going on. Trust me, the McKnights are going to retaliate, and you won't even know when they do. It will be so quiet and discreet that even as you're playing Nancy Drew and looking for clues, you'll completely miss it. You won't find a body this time."

I no longer believed that Phineas was a Bloomfield. The way he spoke of the McKnights—it was with admiration. If their retaliation was going to be so discreet, though, why would he worry about his LA associates coming to town?

Unless this retaliation, whatever it was going to be, involved him and his shop somehow.

What if it wasn't the mayor or the sheriff that ran this town—maybe it was a guy who hid out in a basement all day with burn marks and tattoos covering his arms.

13

I didn't dare look at Benji—for a psychologist, I was terrible at hiding what I was thinking. I liked to believe it helped people trust me, but it also got me into trouble more often than I liked to admit.

"What does Seth think of all this?" I asked Phineas, doubtful that he'd ever talked with the saloon owner at all. If Phineas was a McKnight, as I suspected, why would he share information with a Bloomfield? Unless Seth didn't know of Phineas's familial ties to the town. That was an awfully big assumption, though. Everyone knew everything in a town like this. And moving away to LA wasn't enough to make people forget.

"Same as me. We have felt forced to take sides, even though we really don't want to. We're trying to mediate everything, but it's obviously not working." He looked between Benji and me, then clapped his hands together.

"That's enough about that, though—you didn't come down here for me to bore you to death with town politics. Why don't you follow me to where I melt down the grammium? I can send some home with you as a souvenir."

I wanted to ask more—pry for more information. But a subtle movement in the back of the shop caught my attention. We weren't alone.

My breath hitched when I realized that for someone who had been so guarded when we'd first arrived, Phineas was being awfully accommodating, answering all our questions like this. And he didn't seem to be in a hurry to get rid of us.

"That sounds wonderful, but we've already taken so much of your time." I took a step toward the door. "Thank you for being so accommodating and taking our picture. My daughter is going to lose her mind with envy." I paused, realizing that I sounded way too excited. "I know that sounded awful, but any time I can be the 'cool mom,' I seize the opportunity to show my kids that I'm not too old to have fun."

Phineas laughed. "I understand, and it was no trouble. I don't get a lot of visitors down here."

"That must be lonely. And I'm sure it's difficult, keeping up with all this work on your own."

"Sometimes, but I've always enjoyed being alone with my projects. It's like meditation for me."

Phineas hadn't corrected me that there was someone

else down there with us, which told me all I needed to know.

"Well, we'll let you get back to it, then," I told him, and I tried to play it cool while leading Benji toward the door. He tried to protest, obviously wanting that piece of grammium that Phineas had offered us, but I pretended not to notice.

Walk slow, or he'll know.

Keep your breaths calm.

Don't talk too much, or he'll know you're nervous.

But if you don't talk enough, he'll know something is wrong too.

When Benji and I reached the green door, my husband turned to thank Phineas again, not seeming to notice that anything was amiss, other than me making him leave when he clearly wanted to stay. That was good. If Benji hadn't noticed my sudden surge of anxiety, and he knew me better than anyone, then it was doubtful that Phineas had noticed.

As we pushed the door open and stepped outside, I breathed a sigh of relief.

"Have a nice honeymoon," Phineas said. And then the door slammed shut behind us.

"I can't believe Chuck sent us to where the actual Grammys are made," Benji said, his expression bright. "I mean, I've never been interested in that kind of thing, and yet I suddenly want to watch next award season. Is that crazy?"

I smiled, and I hoped it reached my eyes. "Not crazy at all." I led Benji up the steps and out onto the street.

A sidewalk sign in front of the hotel advertised ghost town tours, and I suddenly couldn't think of anything I'd rather do. Anything to get some space from Dusty Ridge and its family drama.

I'd met dangerous people before, but Phineas scared me more than any of them. He was a master manipulator hiding behind strength, charisma, and Grammy awards.

That was why I'd believed him when he'd said the McKnights could retaliate and we'd never find the body. I'd hazard a guess that he didn't think much of the Bloom-fields and their haphazard way of doing things, and he wanted us to know that his kin would not make the same mistake.

"We said we'd visit a ghost town while we're here," I said, nodding to the sign. "Why don't we go now?"

I hoped it would help me forget that basement and the man in it. But I was doubtful.

"That's a wonderful idea," Benji said, tossing me a smile. It then faltered, like he'd just remembered why we'd come to the hotel in the first place. "I'm sorry, I know we were hoping to find out more about what might have happened to Jeremy. But maybe finding those Grammy awards was the reminder we needed that this is our honey-moon, and the adventures we're meant to have shouldn't involve dead bodies or sheriff's stations. We've done what we can and shouldn't feel guilty about not being able to do more."

"I wholeheartedly agree," I said. "Like Phineas said, no one actually believes that Jeremy left town with the stolen items. That means the sheriff is likely already five steps ahead of us, using her fear and anger as fuel. She will be far more motivated than we could ever be."

It wasn't like me to leave things alone and hope they'd would work out—assume that justice would somehow be served.

But a murderous town feud was not something that even my skills were equipped to handle. Nor did I want to try.

Benji glanced at me, his expression hopeful, but also like he was unsure if I was to be believed. "Did something happen in there?" he asked.

I tilted my head, like I had no idea what he was talking about. I honestly wasn't sure that I did.

"The Grammy shop," he clarified. "It's not like you to rush out of somewhere like that, especially when you knew that I wanted to stay. It almost seemed like you were having a panic attack or something. And now you're suggesting we let the biased sheriff handle this murder investigation while we go on a ghost town tour." He held up his hands in a defensive pose. "Not that I mind. I'm just saying...it's not like you."

Darn. Benji had noticed, he'd just not said anything. And if he had noticed, Phineas probably had as well.

I glanced back toward the green door.

"I'm just a bit tired is all," I said, turning back to Benji. "But I really did love that we followed those crazy directions. It's definitely one of the highlights of our trip."

Benji had noticed where my gaze had landed, and I could tell that he knew I wasn't being entirely truthful.

"You don't trust Phineas?" he asked, his voice low.

I hesitated, then shook my head.

Benji gave me a quizzical look but then nodded, trusting my instinct. "I'm not surprised that you're still recovering from yesterday," he said loudly, smiling and pulling me forward. "Let's see if we can reserve a spot on a ghost town tour for tomorrow morning, and then we'll get some food. I'm starving."

I didn't know what I had done to deserve someone as amazing as Benji, but I was grateful that he'd chosen me to spend his life with. Not many people would put up with my quirks.

After reserving two seats on the tour for the following morning, we headed back to the saloon for lunch. As we crossed the street, I glanced back at the hotel.

I paused.

A man was watching us through a window. When his gaze met mine, he stepped back and let the curtain fall back into place.

"Maddie," Benji called to me, and my gaze jumped to him. He was already several steps ahead of me, and I hurried to join him, not having noticed a car that had been waiting for me to cross the road.

"Sorry," I said. "Someone was watching us."

Benji's forehead scrunched in concern. "Phineas?"

I shook my head. "No, a man on the second floor of the hotel, but I couldn't tell who it was."

It could have been innocent, but I was too paranoid to believe that. Even though Benji and I had made the choice to stop investigating, we would need to be careful for the remainder of our stay. We were on the town's watchlist, and they had eyes everywhere.

14

W hen we arrived back at the saloon, Amy greeted us at the door, but, even though she was polite, she didn't seem particularly excited to see us. Something had changed since the last time we'd spoken. This was further evidenced when we asked to have lunch brought up to our room and the suggestion seemed to make her uneasy. She asked if we would mind eating in the dining room instead.

Benji and I exchanged curious glances but agreed.

"How has your morning been?" Amy asked, leading us through the crowded restaurant to a table in the back corner. The cheerfulness in her voice didn't reach her eyes.

"It's been adventurous, to say the least," I said. "Never a dull moment in this town."

Amy's unease seemed to intensify at my answer, but I pretended not to notice as I took my seat.

After handing us our menus, Amy surprised me by bending in close, her voice dropping in volume. Even though I had to strain to hear what she said, I could feel the power behind her words. She was scared.

"You two need to be careful," she whispered. "If you truly are here for your honeymoon, and even if you aren't, you need to act like it. Rumors are spreading about you two, and in a place like this, that's very dangerous."

"Because we found a body that everyone else wanted to disappear," I said matter-of-factly.

Amy froze, a look of horror on her face, before she whipped out a notebook from her pocket. "Like I said, you need to act like you're here on your honeymoon and not as investigative reporters. For all our sakes."

Benji tilted his head to the side. "What do you mean by that?"

She hesitated, like she was trying to find the right words. "My dad tells me I have a trusting nature and I see the good in everyone," she said, her words slow. "And that's not necessarily a bad thing. Until it is. He says it's going to get me killed someday."

I shared a concerned look with Benji before resting a hand on Amy's arm. She stilled. "You don't need to worry about us," I said. "We don't trust as easily as it appears."

"I wasn't talking about you trusting others," Amy said. "I was talking about me trusting *you*."

I opened my mouth but couldn't find the words.

Amy released a long sigh. "It has been suggested that my dad and I would do well to request you find new accommodations—that we need to protect ourselves from appearing too friendly with you. My dad agrees—but I don't. The thing is, if I ask you to leave, you won't find another place in town that will let you stay. I can tell you're good people, but you're not making this easy on me when you're snooping around and getting involved in our local affairs. So, like I said, please be the honeymooners that you are supposed to be. Otherwise, you're going to need to find another town to honeymoon in."

Local affairs. Meaning a murder investigation that the town would like to keep in-house.

"We have two seats reserved on the ghost town tour first thing in the morning," I assured her, "and we have every intention of being the honeymooners that we should have been this entire time."

Amy didn't look convinced—she thought we were going to cause trouble and she'd end up in the thick of it. Regardless, she gave a slight nod. "Good. I'm glad to hear it."

"That being said," I continued, "is there anyone in particular we need to be careful around?"

My thoughts immediately jumped to the Grammy shop.

Amy pretended to be taking our order in her notebook. "Sure. Everyone."

"Including Phineas?"

Amy's hand stilled. "You've met Phineas? I heard that Chuck tried sending you guys over there but you hadn't gone."

"We just got back," Benji said. "We thought it was pretty cool that the Grammys are made in a random basement in the middle of an old Western town." Realization spread across his expression, and he groaned. "They aren't real Grammys, are they? They are a cover."

"Oh, they're the real deal," Amy said. "Crazy as that is. But it's not a tourist attraction, and Phineas doesn't advertise what he does there. That doesn't stop Chuck from pranking Phineas and sending tourists to his shop, though. Those two have a weird friendship, and even though it drives Phineas crazy, I think he secretly likes it." She paused. "Of course, Phineas knows by now that you two aren't our average tourists."

Benji's gaze whipped to me. "You knew something was off, didn't you, when you were rushing us out of the shop."

"I didn't suspect anything at the beginning," I said. "But when Phineas was talking to us about the feud, I saw someone in the back. I don't know who it was, they were taking pains to not be seen, but Phineas said he was there alone when he obviously wasn't."

Benji released a hard breath. "And I missed it all. He seemed like someone who was concerned about his town but who also just wanted to be left alone to make his Grammys. That seemed like a reasonable thing to ask."

"He's all those things," Amy said. "And so much more. You're right that Phineas doesn't work alone. Jeremy used to work for him, until Phineas fired him. And right when Jeremy was trying to build a better life for himself. And for me." Amy shook her head. "I wouldn't be surprised if Phineas was the one who convinced Jeremy to rob the bank. It would be just like him, leaving Jeremy in a vulnerable position without a job, and then showing him the door to easy money."

"So, what, Jeremy and Phineas hatch this plan together, and they agree to split it fifty-fifty?" Benji asked. "If Phineas is as slippery as you say he is, why would Jeremy trust him with a deal like that?"

"Because Phineas isn't just slippery," Amy said. "He's dangerous. And you don't turn him down. My bet is that Jeremy planned on riding straight out of town with those valuables and never coming back. His plan was to disappear."

"He had no idea it was a setup," I said quietly. "Phineas would have known that Jeremy would leave with the valuables, and there is only that one road out of here. Further down the road, Phineas is all ready to steal the bags from Jeremy, and then get rid of the evidence."

"The evidence," Amy said. "Meaning Jeremy."

Well, this day had taken a turn for the worse. That Grammy shop was still one of the coolest things I'd ever seen, but it would forever be tied to Phineas and the murder of Jeremy McKnight.

The three of us turned when the door to the saloon swung open, mostly because of the abnormally slow gait of the visitor.

Sheriff McKnight.

It was like she was trying to make up for her short stature by exaggerating her steady stride, just like they did in the old Westerns.

Her gaze landed on us, and she walked over.

"I was hoping you'd be here," she said, eyeing us.

"Did you find something?" I asked, hopeful. I wanted nothing more than for Phineas to be arrested, justice to be served, and Benji and I to be able to finish our honeymoon in peace.

"More like heard something. We received an anonymous call."

The way she said it, it made me uneasy. "What did you hear?"

"That someone had stashed something related to Jeremy's disappearance here at the saloon. Your hotel room, to be more precise."

Benji, Amy, and I all shared alarmed looks.

"You'll need a search warrant," Amy started, but Sheriff McKnight was already ahead of her, pulling out the warrant as she spoke.

"You'll find everything is in order," the sheriff said, extending it to Amy.

Amy didn't bother to take it, her gaze steady on the

sheriff. "How did you get it so fast? No one ever pays attention to Dusty Ridge—it takes weeks for anything to get done."

Sheriff McKnight raised a shoulder. "A judge owed me a favor."

"You mean he lost to you in poker," Amy said with a frown.

The sheriff was quiet for a moment, her gaze intense. "I have to drive three hours every month to attend a poker game that I despise, just so I can take care of my town. But if that's what is required to get anyone to pay attention to us, then I will make that drive and play the game. I have a few favors saved up, and catching Jeremy's killer made the top of the list of my priorities. I don't see anything wrong with that."

"Would you have used that favor if it had been my dad who had gone missing, rather than your brother?" Amy countered.

Things were getting heated, and I really would have preferred not to be here for it. I slid my seat back, ready to go literally anywhere else. We could eat later.

"Hold up," Sheriff McKnight said, raising her hand. "You're going to sit back down until we finish our search."

That was when I realized that it wasn't just Amy and Seth who were suspects in Jeremy's disappearance. Despite having no motive, Benji and I were under suspicion as well.

Or at least, that was what the sheriff wanted us to think.

I hadn't even noticed Deputy Steve go upstairs, but he exited the elevator a short moment later, a grim expression on his face. "I found the noose," he said, holding up the bundle of rope. "It was in the closet upstairs."

15

B enji and I stared at the sheriff. My mind was blank, unable to process what we were hearing.

"We didn't kill Jeremy," Benji protested. "That's ridiculous. We'd only been in town for a few hours when we found his body—why would we have killed someone we didn't know, and then tell you about it? Did we tell him to rob the bank too?" He turned to Amy, as if she could do anything about it. "You know this is insane, right?"

Amy turned an angry glare on the sheriff. "Of course it is. You are obviously being set up."

Sheriff McKnight seemed pleased at how things were turning out. I had liked the sheriff when we'd first met, but she was taking far too much pleasure in Amy's discomfort.

"And who would set them up?" the sheriff asked. "Perhaps my brother's bitter ex-girlfriend, who wanted revenge but needed someone to take the fall."

"I wasn't his ex-girlfriend; we never broke up," she said, folding her arms over her chest. "He just told you we did so you'd stop telling him to dump me every time you saw him."

Was it possible that the sheriff was setting Benji and me up so she could ultimately set Amy up? There would be no love lost between those two.

"Hold up," I said, releasing an ear-splitting whistle. I turned to ask Deputy Steve where exactly he'd found the noose, but he was no longer in the room with us. "Where's Steve?"

"Right here," he said, poking his head around the front door. And then he walked in—leading a horse.

"Get that thing out of my restaurant," Amy screeched, rushing forward. "You know I could be shut down for having an animal in here." She grabbed the lead from the deputy's hand and pushed the horse back outside.

"Is that—" Sheriff McKnight started.

Steve nodded. "Jeremy's horse, Bullet. He was in the stable out back, exactly where Jeremy would have put him after the bank robbery."

The sheriff's gaze landed on the front door. "You just allowed one of our prime suspects to walk off with an important piece of evidence. She might, in fact, already be using that horse to ride out of town, considering—"

"I was just tying it up on the hitching post," Amy said, walking back in with a frown. "I wasn't trying to make a run for it. My dad and I are innocent. I don't know how

Bullet got back in the stable, but anyone could have placed him there."

"You have security cameras?" Sheriff McKnight asked, taking a step toward Amy.

"Behind the saloon? Of course not," she snapped. "Why would we?"

The sheriff raised her shoulders as if to say, *What do you expect me to do in this situation?*

And then she stepped toward Amy and pulled out her handcuffs. "Amy Bloomfield, you'll want to put up your closed sign, because I am arresting you for the murder of Jeremy McKnight." The sheriff glanced toward Benji and me. "Which means that you'll need to find new accommodations."

Accommodations that Amy had said we wouldn't find.

"You can't prove anything," Amy insisted. "I didn't put the noose in that closet upstairs or put the horse in the stable. You can't even prove that Jeremy is dead."

"And yet, we know that if his horse is here, then he didn't make it out of town like you tried to make it seem," Sheriff McKnight said. She motioned for Amy to turn, and then she slapped the handcuffs on the poor woman.

"Tell my dad what has happened," Amy called over her shoulder as she was led outside. "He'll know what to do."

I didn't get the chance to ask where he was before Amy and the sheriff disappeared outside.

"You'll find him at the museum," Deputy Steve said. "If he's not here, he's there. Always."

The thought made me sad—maybe one day Seth would get that position at the museum that he'd always wanted. Until then, he seemed to be doomed to wander it, remembering the good days and hoping for better ones.

I was grateful for the excuse to leave the saloon, though —I really didn't want to be there without Amy. Without her presence, it felt hollow.

Benji and I hurried down the street, but when we turned the corner to go to the museum in search of Seth, I stopped.

"You okay?" Benji asked, immediately taking my arm, just in case I were to fall again. I waved him off.

"I'm fine. It's just that every time we visit this part of town, something terrible happens. The first time we were here, we discovered a body. The second time, I was physically attacked. I'm not hopeful that this time will be any different, considering we're about to tell Seth that his daughter has been arrested for murder."

"But we're just the messengers," Benji said.

"Everyone shoots the messenger," I pointed out, but resumed walking. Amy had said that Seth would know what to do, and we needed to trust that.

When we entered the museum, I expected we'd be interrupting another argument between Seth and the museum's docent, Peggy. But instead, it was eerily quiet.

"Hello," I called, stopping at the front desk.

A thud came from somewhere in the back of the museum. I shot Benji a worried look.

"See?" I whispered. "Nothing good ever comes from visiting this museum."

Benji looked equally concerned, but instead of retreating, he entered the exhibit room. I followed him into a room filled with a variety of old pistols and cowboy hats that marked the passage of time, showing how they had changed over the decades.

"Why is the museum so dark?" I asked, noticing how most of the overhead lights seemed to be either turned off or burned out.

"Because the museum is closed, and the front door was supposed to be locked," Peggy said, stepping from around one of the exhibits. She threw an annoyed glance behind her, like someone else had been at fault for that. Her sudden appearance startled me so much that I tripped over Benji's foot when I turned, and I nearly fell into a glass display case.

Once I recovered, I glanced at my phone. "It's only two o'clock," I said. "You're supposed to be open for another five hours."

"We closed early," Peggy said, stubbornly crossing her arms over her chest. "For a staff meeting. So, if you don't mind—"

Benji walked around her. "You're the only one who works here."

I was surprised at Benji's bluntness, he wasn't usually the type, but if there was ever a need for the direct approach, now was the time.

"We have several volunteers—" Peggy started to say.

"We're looking for Seth," I interrupted, following Benji's lead.

Benji walked around the exhibit toward the back of the museum but stopped short, causing me to collide with him.

"Benji, what are you—" My words cut off when I saw a small table set up in the middle of the museum, a chair on each side. And Seth was in one of those chairs. He gave us an embarrassed smile, followed by a little wave. "Just taking my lunch break. Sometimes I need to get away from the saloon, and the museum calms me."

It seemed it was more than just the museum that calmed him. Judging by the setup of the food on the table, this was a date.

"I thought you two don't like each other," I said as Peggy joined Seth at the table. "You were arguing so terribly about the stolen noose."

"Only people who care about each other argue the way we do," Seth said, tossing Peggy a look of admiration. It was more than that, though—the man was in love with the museum docent.

"But she took your job," I protested.

"And I was furious about it," Seth said. "But I've found that I like the current circumstances better. I can come and go as I please, and Peggy asks my advice about the exhibits. When I'm here, I put on a volunteer vest and answer the tourists' questions, but then I leave when I get tired. Peggy—she never runs out of energy, so we work well together."

Peggy's lips twitched up at the edges at the compliment, but then she looked to Benji and me and her eyes narrowed. "If you speak of this to anyone—"

"Pegs, you don't need to threaten them. They are good people," Seth interrupted. He gave us an apologetic smile. "You already know about the animosity that's been brewing between our two families. We figured it was best to keep things quiet for right now."

So, both father and daughter were dating someone from the other family.

Amy. I'd almost forgotten.

"We don't care that you're having lunch with Peggy," I said. "We came to tell you that Amy has been arrested. Someone planted the missing noose in the closet of our suite upstairs, as well as Jeremy's horse in your stable. Sheriff McKnight is convinced that Amy is her brother's killer."

Seth leaped from his chair. "Tess knows that Amy wouldn't do something like that. If she thought one of us had killed Jeremy, it would be me."

"You think she arrested Amy so you would come in and confess to killing Jeremy?" I asked. After what I'd seen earlier, I'd believe anything in this messed-up town. With every hour, Dusty Ridge seemed more like the actual Wild West from the 1800s, and that was not a good thing. A place where people took the law into their own hands and families feuded over minor slights was not the kind of place that should still exist in the world.

"That's exactly what I think," Seth said.

Benji spoke up, though he seemed hesitant to do so. "Seth, your daughter said that you would know what to do. What did she mean by that?"

Seth froze, his gaze leaping to Peggy. "You don't think she meant—"

Peggy lifted a shoulder. "I can't imagine she did, but with how things have been going lately, who knows."

Seth groaned and shook his head.

"What does she want you to do?" I asked.

"Our family has an old protocol that dates back almost two hundred years," Seth said. "If someone was in trouble, and there didn't seem to be any way out, they would challenge the offender to a duel. In this case, it would be Sheriff McKnight."

Benji and I stared.

"You're serious?" Benji asked. "A duel. Like, walk ten paces, turn around and shoot?"

Seth nodded. "I'm afraid so. It hasn't been used for over a century, but we never bothered to change it in the law books. We didn't think we needed to—it is so antiquated."

"You're not going to actually go through with it, though, are you?" Peggy asked.

"What choice do I have? My daughter has been wrongly accused—set up by the offending party. They'll never let her go. Even Amy knew—this is the only way."

16

B enji, Peggy, and I tried to reason with Seth as he speed-walked toward the sheriff's station, but no amount of begging or reasoning could change Seth's mind.

"You do know that this is insane, right?" Peggy asked, struggling to keep up. "You can't challenge the sheriff to a duel."

"Is it antiquated?" Seth asked. "Of course. Is it barbaric? Without a doubt. But you know as well as I do that things have gotten out of control between our families. Amy and I were set up for the murder of Jeremy McKnight, and we don't know how many people are behind it. If the sheriff thinks I will admit to something I didn't do, she has another thing coming. I'd rather die for Amy than do that."

We really were back in the 1800s.

When we reached the sheriff's office, Seth burst through the front door, startling Deputy Steve. "Where is she?" Seth demanded when he didn't see the sheriff. "Tess," he yelled. "I need to talk to you."

"Sheriff McKnight isn't—" Deputy Steve started, but the sheriff stepped out from the back and laid a hand on Steve's shoulder.

"It's all right. I've been expecting Seth."

"I'm sure you have," Seth said. "What you probably didn't expect, however, was that I am challenging you to a duel."

"Are you kidding me?" a woman screeched from the back of the sheriff's station. "Dad, have you lost your mind?"

Apparently, this was also where they had Amy locked up, somewhere in a cell at the back of the station.

"Yes, he has," Peggy called back. "Will you talk some sense into him?"

If Sheriff McKnight was surprised by Seth's declaration, she was very good at hiding it. Instead, she seemed thoroughly amused by the idea of it. "A duel," she mused. "I have to say, that's a first for me."

"Amy is innocent," Seth growled. "I know you won't let her go of your own accord, so I need to settle this the only way I know how."

"Dad, stop it," Amy called again from the back. "You're going to get yourself killed."

"It's okay, honey," Seth called back. "You told the honeymooners that I would know what to do about the situation—and this is it."

A groan.

"I meant that you'd know to call Uncle Mike."

Seth's angry expression melted into surprise. "Oh. I suppose that would make more sense." He turned to Benji and me. "Mike is my brother who moved to Denver after finishing law school. I hear he's quite good."

I didn't know whether to laugh or cry with relief.

"Do you still want that duel?" Sheriff McKnight asked. She was half the height of Seth, but her gaze challenged him. She was not afraid.

"I suppose not," Seth said, though he seemed disappointed. "But what is it going to take for you to release Amy? Sure, you found the missing noose and Jeremy's horse at the saloon, but how would your anonymous caller know that the noose was in an upstairs closet if they hadn't planted it themselves? Only we and our guests have access to that elevator."

Seth realized what he'd just said, and his and the sheriff's gazes swiveled to Benji and me.

"Don't look at us," Benji said. "We didn't make the anonymous call."

Sheriff McKnight's gaze returned to Seth. "I'm sorry, but there's only so much I can do."

"Suspecting someone of a crime isn't enough to arrest them," he protested.

"No, but finding the noose and horse at your establishment is. That's called physical evidence," Sheriff McKnight said. "Which reminds me..." She turned to the deputy. "Go ahead."

Deputy Steve hesitated, and it was apparent that he didn't like what he was being asked to do.

"Now," the sheriff prodded.

The deputy opened the counter and stepped through. "Sorry about this, Seth. But I have to arrest you too. Being like you said—that saloon belongs to both you and Amy."

"Wait a minute," Peggy protested as Steve led Seth into the back of the station. "I can attest to his whereabouts on the day of Jeremy's disappearance."

"Don't you worry, Peggy. I'm going to get all the sordid details of your fling when I'm corroborating Seth's alibi," the sheriff said. When Peggy's eyebrows popped up in surprise, Sheriff McKnight laughed. "The whole town knows about what's going on between you and Seth, but that doesn't mean he didn't find the time to kill Jeremy before, or after, meeting up with you at the museum."

Peggy didn't have a retort to that and frowned, crossing her arms in front of her chest and letting her glare do the talking.

"This is all such a mess," I said. "Does no one trust anyone, even within the same family?"

"We used to," Peggy said. "But no, no one trusts anyone. Even the sheriff. Which is a shame, because I voted for you, Tess. You were good people. And somehow this town got to you. Otherwise, you wouldn't be arresting Seth and Amy when you know that they're innocent. I guess you have a duty to keep the family happy, though." Peggy turned to Benji and me. "I'm sorry you got caught up in all of it. If I were you, I'd pack your bags and honeymoon somewhere else. You deserve somewhere nice."

Sheriff McKnight shook her head. "I'm afraid they are witnesses, and suspects, in this whole thing too." When she saw I was about to protest, she held up a hand. "That doesn't mean I'm going to be arresting you and your husband, but you two were the ones who discovered the body in the woods, and the presumed murder weapon was found in your hotel room. I can't ignore that." She turned back to Peggy. "I'm sorry you don't think I'm worthy of my position anymore. Believe it or not, I don't answer to the family—I answer to justice. A man—my brother—is assumed dead, and the murder weapon, as well as his horse, were found at the saloon. That's where the evidence is leading me. The fact that Seth was at the museum on the day of Jeremy's disappearance isn't an alibi—it places him at the assumed crime scene. You'll want to pray that we don't find the stolen valuables at the saloon. If we do, I'm not sure there is much hope for Seth or Amy. And I do like both of them. A lot."

"You have a funny way of showing it," Peggy said with a scowl.

The sheriff shook her head. "Look, I'm not blind. I know that my brother was...difficult. And Amy put up with him for a lot longer than she should have. That's why I encouraged him to break up with her—to spare her. I'm also very aware that their complicated relationship could be used against Seth and Amy if they ever go to trial. If they didn't kill Jeremy, I need to find who did. Before it's too late."

I wasn't perfect at reading people, but the sheriff seemed sincere. She believed what she was saying.

I placed a hand on Peggy's arm. "I'm sorry, but there doesn't seem to be anything we can do for either one of them right now."

I nodded toward the door, indicating that we should leave. Peggy gave a numb nod, threw a last glance toward the back of the station where the deputy had taken Seth, then followed me outside.

"Amy said that Seth should have called his brother, Mike. Do you have his number?" I asked Peggy, stopping on the sidewalk next to the sheriff's car.

Peggy shook her head. "No, but I can find someone who does. It's not going to do much good, though. Seth's opinion of his brother is elevated—Mike is an idiot. They'd be better off having you as a lawyer than bringing him up from Denver."

Peggy's comment caught me off guard, and I tried not to laugh at the blunt way she spoke of Seth's brother. "All right, then. I guess that means it is up to us, because right now all the evidence points to Amy and Seth, with Benji and me as the backup contenders. With odds like that, I'd rather not put our fate in the hands of Seth's brother."

Peggy studied me for a moment, and when Benji

nodded his agreement, she gave a shake of her head. "I've never met two people like you—and certainly not tourists like you. But if you want to help, who am I to say no?"

"Great," I said. "What do we know about what happened the night Jeremy died? Assuming that he is dead."

Peggy glanced around uneasily. "Not here. Let's go back to the museum."

Something—or someone—had her spooked. Benji and I followed her around the corner to the museum, and as soon as we were inside, Peggy locked the front door.

"The night of Jeremy's disappearance," she started, "I knew that boy hadn't skipped town. He did his bank robbery the same as every afternoon, and I heard him bring the horse around the woods. That's where he'd go, you know. Far enough around the bend in the road that folks could no longer see him, and then he'd bring the horse around through the woods and come out right here."

"That sounds like where we found him hanging," I mused.

Peggy nodded. "That's what I thought too."

"And he came through the woods, same as usual that day?" Benji asked.

"Like clockwork. He rides into the woods, changes out of his costume, then hops back on his horse and rides into this clearing and around to the back of the bank, where he returns the prop and costume so that it can be cleaned.

There are two sets of costumes, and he exchanges the dirty set for a clean one."

I walked over to the front desk and leaned against it. "And you're sure he made it to the clearing?"

"I told you I'm sure, didn't I? I always ask him to stay clear of the movie sets, but he insists on jumping the fence and riding straight through them because it's a shortcut. It scares the tourists who decided to skip the show, but Jeremy always said that if they don't go to the show, the show comes to them."

Peggy chuckled, like that annoyance was a fond memory.

I tapped my fingers on the counter. "Okay, we know that Jeremy was alive that afternoon and that he never left town. If he exchanges his costume at the bank, why did he change into the clean one that evening?"

"And did Jeremy rob the bank during the show, or did the valuables disappear later on?" Benji asked.

I glanced at Peggy. "Who started the rumor that Jeremy had robbed the bank and left town?"

Peggy shifted uncomfortably from one foot to the other. She obviously wanted to help Seth and Amy, but turning on her family and neighbors was difficult for someone in the best of circumstances, let alone for something like this.

"You could be saving two lives," Benji gently coaxed.

Peggy hesitated. "The manager of the bank, Kennedy, said

that he saw Jeremy leave the bank during the show with three prop bags of money. Normally he only has one, because that's fewer bags they have to clean and keep track of, but Jeremy had been insisting for months that it wasn't realistic for a bank robber to ride off with less than three or four bags of cash."

"And then when Jeremy went missing, along with fifty thousand dollars' worth of valuables, it was assumed that he'd taken off with it during the show," I finished. "How long was it until both he and the valuables were discovered missing?"

"Kennedy always checks the tills, the vault, and all that, before he leaves for the day. Must have been around four-thirty or five. He noticed that several of the safety deposit boxes had been left out, and they were empty with no record that the owners had been in that day. So, of course, he called for the sheriff. It turned out that someone had used a drill to open them."

I glanced at Benji. "Seems pretty suspicious that someone would steal that much stuff, then leave all evidence of it sitting out there in the open. Why wouldn't he return the boxes to where they belonged? It would delay the discovery of the missing contents."

He nodded. "It was like he wanted to be caught."

Peggy glanced between us. "What are you saying—that someone else had wanted it to look like Jeremy had taken them?"

"That's exactly what we're saying," I said. "But who

would have had access to the vault, other than the bank manager?"

Peggy shrugged. "No one. There is usually only one teller on duty, and the teller doesn't have that kind of access. Ever since the safety deposit keys were stolen last year, Kennedy doesn't trust anyone. And for good reason— it had been a teller who had taken them."

"It seems too easy," I murmured. "No way would your bank manager be dumb enough to stage a robbery at his own bank—he would be the first person that people would suspect." I glanced up. "Who was it that stole the safety deposit keys last year?"

If Peggy had been uncomfortable before, it was nothing compared to now. She remained quiet, but her gaze flitted to the window. I glanced over and saw Chuck trimming some bushes outside the museum with hedge clippers.

"Peggy, I'm sorry, but we have to talk to him."

She nodded once, but she didn't move to follow Benji and me outside.

It was clear: This was one conversation we were going to need to have on our own.

17

W hen Benji and I walked out of the museum and approached Chuck, he didn't stop trimming. If anything, he was more focused.

"Hey, Chuck," I said.

He ignored me.

"We followed your directions over to the hotel," I tried again.

That gave him pause.

Chuck glanced my way, his gaze wary. "What did you two think of it?" he asked, snipping each branch so it was perfectly in line with the branch next to it.

"Amazing," Benji answered. Even though it had turned out that Phineas was supposedly a super dangerous guy, it hadn't taken away from the fact that we had held actual Grammy awards. "I never expected we could find something like that in a hotel basement."

Chuck's lips quirked up, and it seemed he was trying his hardest not to talk to us. He lost the battle, spinning toward us. "I just knew you were going to love it. You saw the award that Taylor Swift broke, right? Even though I've been down in that basement a hundred times, it never gets old."

"You recognize the unique aspects of your town—you understand what it is that makes it special. And valuable," I said. "And you like to share that with others."

"Oh, I sure do. We have plenty of things that make this town special. Take this museum, for instance," he said, nodding toward the building next to us. "These aren't just old ropes and guns and cowboy hats. Can you imagine being on these old movie sets back in the day, and meeting the type of men and women who handled these props? It's incredible."

"Is that why you took this job after leaving the bank?" Benji asked.

I wanted to whack him on the arm. There was a way to do these investigations—a subtle way we had to go about it —otherwise we'd never get the information we needed.

And that was not it.

Except, Chuck didn't seem to mind at all. Instead, he nodded vigorously. "Absolutely. I wasn't meant to be a guy wearing a suit and tie and helping people get their money out of the bank. Money—it's irrelevant. Pointless. What good is money in a place like this—a place that's rich in history and friendship? I thank my lucky stars every day that I get to live in a town like Dusty Ridge."

I tilted my head to the side, confused. Chuck really didn't seem to care about money. At all.

"We heard that you'd stolen the safety deposit keys," Benji said, equally confused.

Chuck's expression opened up in delight. "Oh, good. I was hoping that rumor would stick." He waved a hand through the air. "Naw, I only lost them. Honestly, now don't go telling anyone this, but I quit my job—just couldn't stand coming in anymore. I thought that getting fired would make me appear tougher, though, so that's the story I asked Kennedy to pass around. You start telling people that you don't like money, and they think you're crazy."

Chuck was an interesting person. Charismatic, wanted to be seen as tough, but really just had a good heart. It made it difficult to believe he had anything to do with Jeremy's disappearance.

"Were the keys ever found?" I asked.

"Yup," he said. "They went missing for a couple of days, and then suddenly showed back up at the sheriff's station—turned in by someone who found them on the walkway."

"And you told Kennedy to tell people it had been you who had taken them," Benji said.

Chuck nodded.

"Did you ever have access to the vault?" I asked.

"Yeah," Chuck said. "I had to...back then, Kennedy wasn't always around."

"And now?"

"He doesn't even take sick days."

I took a moment to think on that. "Jeremy came in to rob the bank every day for the show," I said, slowly. "Did Kennedy have any problems with Jeremy?" I asked the question out of obligation. Kennedy would have to be the dumbest thief in the world if it really had been him.

"Of course," Chuck said. "Most people did. But I'll tell you what I told the sheriff. That kid had potential, and he was starting to realize it. I'd bet if he'd had another couple years, people wouldn't have even recognized him. That's what epiphanies do to people, and Jeremy had a big one."

"What kind of epiphany?" Benji asked.

"Well," Chuck said, leaning forward as if he had a secret, even though he didn't bother to lower his voice. "I'm sure you heard how Jeremy was driving drunk a few months back and destroyed the front part of the saloon. He'd come roaring down the street and didn't even touch the brake until he was already halfway through the front window. After that, the man was inconsolable for days, knowing that he could have easily killed Amy or Seth. Honestly, he probably wasn't all that worried about Seth—the two have never seen eye to eye—but knowing that he could have killed Amy—he became a different man. I didn't see Jeremy touch a single drop of alcohol after that point. For all of Jeremy's faults, he wasn't a violent person—never got into a bar fight, and certainly never lifted a hand against Amy—no matter what people say."

That would explain why the saloon looked like it had gone through recent renovations.

"Did anyone else know about this epiphany?" I asked. If plenty of people had ill feelings toward Jeremy, a sudden moment of clarity would likely not be enough to erase years of injustices. Maybe driving through the front of the saloon had been the final act that had sent someone over the edge.

"Jeremy tried to tell people he was a changed man, but I'm fairly certain Amy was the only one who believed him. And me. I could see the change—it was a night and day difference."

Chuck seemed to have a very high opinion of himself and his own moral character. He had made a point to ensure we knew that he didn't care about money and that he was one of the only people in town to see Jeremy's potential—it was almost like he was telling us what he wanted us to hear, and I wondered how much of it was actually true.

"Thank you so much for your time," I told Chuck. "You've really helped us to see how special the people in this town are."

Chuck practically glowed at the compliment. "I'm happy to help in any way I can. You think of anything else, you come back. I'm always happy to send you off on a new adventure, if you have the time. The Grammy shop was just the beginning."

"We'll keep that kind offer in mind," I told him, knowing full well that we had our hands full of adventure and we really didn't need any more of it.

"What do you think?" Benji asked as we walked back into the museum.

I released a slow breath. "I think Chuck is a man who is so desperate to be liked that he will spin his story in whichever way he thinks will present him in the best light. He wants us to think he is morally superior to everyone else in this town, which means he likely doesn't think much of the people here. I don't know that that means he would rob the bank and kill someone, though."

"You think he told us the truth about the safety deposit keys?"

I hesitated, because I was in no way a human lie detector. "I think so."

Benji seemed defeated at the news. "So, where does that leave us?"

"I guess we could talk to that bank manager," I said, not sounding in the least convincing. Honestly, I didn't think it would lead to anything, and Benji could tell.

"We need to find those stolen items," he said. "It's the only way to prove that Amy and Seth didn't do it. But I think you're right—the bank manager isn't going to have them. Maybe the teller?"

I blew out a hard breath and rubbed my eyebrows. No

one robbed banks anymore. There was too much risk, considering how advanced security had gotten nowadays.

"What security did the bank have?" I asked. "Cameras? A security guard?"

Benji looked intrigued. "Now that's an interesting question and warrants a visit to the bank. Maybe the manager didn't steal the items, but surely he should have an idea of how the burglar did it."

"Hey, Peggy," I called, wondering where she'd gone while we'd been talking with Chuck. I wanted to say goodbye, but she wasn't in the lobby or at the desk.

No answer from the museum.

"She must be in the far back," Benji said. "We can catch up with her later."

Benji and I left the museum, waved goodbye to Chuck, and walked back to Main Street. I glanced in the window of the sheriff's office as we passed and saw Deputy Steve leaning on the counter, his gaze fixed straight ahead. Our gazes met, and I waved. He frowned and gave a tentative wave back. I wondered if he felt weird being friendly with us, considering we were technically murder suspects.

"After you," Benji said, holding the bank's door open, allowing me to enter in front of him. The inside was nice and certainly had that old bank feeling, but it was also very cramped. A counter ran along the side of the narrow building, and metal bars rose from the counter, protecting the teller, with only a small window on the bottom for the exchange of money to occur. Bank robberies had been a normal thing in the Wild West, and it seemed this was the only way they had to protect themselves against it.

"Welcome to the bank," a young woman in a historical dress said from behind the counter. She was partially hidden behind the bars, and I hadn't even noticed her. She tucked a lock of blonde hair behind one ear before launching into a spiel about the history of banking. It seemed that in Dusty Ridge, regardless of your employment, you had to both do your job and be a tour guide.

"In the nineteenth century," she said, "most people didn't trust banks. Often merchants would handle their own lines of credit with their customers, allowing farmers to pay when their crops came in for the season."

That confirmed my theory about bank robbing being a normal fact of life. Why trust a bank if you had no assurances that your money wouldn't be stolen?

"What kind of security measures, besides these bars, did the banks have in place?" Benji asked.

The young women smiled. "I'm so glad you asked. There was a large metal vault that would make it difficult for bank robbers to access the money. However, if you had a gun to your head, it wouldn't take much convincing to go back and open the vault yourself."

Made sense.

"Has your town added any security measures to prevent that from happening?" I asked. "I know Dusty Ridge is supposed to be straight out of a history book, but it seems that you'd do some things to keep up with the modern times."

The young woman's smile never dropped, and she kept her historian's tone. "In our quest to be as authentic as possible, we have no alarms, though we did add one security camera. I hope you'll excuse the departure from authenticity."

I grimaced. "Has anyone else asked that question before," I glanced at her name tag, "Claudia?"

Her smile still firmly in place, she shook her head. "No, they haven't."

"Okay, good. Please don't tell anyone else that you don't have alarms. We were asking because we were curious, but others might not have such innocent intentions."

Claudia's expression dropped, as if she'd just realized what she'd done. "Oh my gosh, I'm so sorry." She lowered her voice. "You won't tell my boss, right?"

I smiled. "No, we won't tell Kennedy. If someone does ever ask that question, you can just tell them that the bank has taken all necessary precautions to keep both its staff and its customers, and their money, safe."

She nodded slowly. "Isn't that lying?"

Technically, yes. But it was better than the truth.

"No, not at all. You're keeping things vague."

Claudia brightened. "Oh yes, of course. Thank you for your insight."

"Now, this is as an investigator, and not as a tourist," I

said. "But are you able to access historical security footage, if the need were to arise?"

Claudia nodded. "Yes, of course."

"That means you could access footage from the day of Jeremy McKnight's disappearance, correct? We're trying to help figure out what really happened that day."

Claudia's lips parted in surprise, and she nodded slowly. "Yes, but there is no audio. And the sheriff has already looked it over. In fact, the tape is likely still with her."

"Tape?" Benji asked, confused.

I bent my head and rubbed my eyebrows. Their security camera recorded onto a VHS tape. And if their security system still used VHS tapes, they'd record over everything with new footage once it filled up. They might have done some updates, but they certainly weren't modern, not since the 1990s.

"Thank you for your time," I said, turning to leave. There was no way Sheriff McKnight was going to give us access to that tape.

"If you want, I can tell you what I saw," Claudia said as I opened the door.

I paused and turned back. And here I considered myself an investigator. I hadn't even thought that the teller might have seen something. But of course she had. She would have been here during the staged robbery.

"Did you see Jeremy that day?" Benji asked.

She nodded, her expression somber. "Yes, I did. I was one of the last people to see him alive, God rest his soul."

"When he brought back the bank bags and his costume?"

Claudia brightened, like she was excited to share exclusive information with us. "No. Strangely enough, he didn't return them that day. It was during the show that I saw him."

"And you're sure it was Jeremy who robbed the bank during the show?"

"Oh, it sure was. He gave me his signature wink that he gives me every afternoon as he's demanding the money—he acts all tough when he's holding up the bank, but he likes to let me know that it's not as serious as all that. No one else would know about the wink."

I shared a confused glance with Benji.

"And you're the one who gave him his usual prop bags during the show?" I asked.

"Now that you mention—" The young woman paused, and then a horrified expression crossed her face. "Oh, no. I did something terrible, didn't I?"

18

C laudia looked like she was going to have a panic attack, her breaths coming sharp and fast.

"You didn't do anything wrong," I said, leaning on the counter and forcing her to meet my gaze. "Just tell us what happened."

She gave a quick nod, trying to hold back the tears. "There were two extra bags this time, but I assumed they were there to add to the drama. Jeremy had been saying for months that no robber is going to steal one bag of cash— why not make it more? He and his horse could handle it, he said. So, when there were three bags set behind my counter, I thought they were props for the show. I mean, they all had that comically large dollar sign on them— there was no difference between them. And you should have seen how Jeremy's eyes lit up when I handed him the extra bags. He thought that people had finally listened to him." She lowered her voice, as if telling us a secret. "No one ever listened to Jeremy. The only reason he got the job in the show was because he's the sheriff's brother. And no one fit the bill of outlaw better than Jeremy."

All right, then.

"And you have no idea who placed the extra bags behind the counter?" Benji asked. "Who would normally do it?"

"Usually, I do. After Jeremy returns the bag, it's kept on a table at the back of the bank, and I grab it a few minutes before the show. If for some reason I'm busy with a customer, Kennedy, my boss, grabs it for me. This time, however, the bags were already behind the counter, filled and waiting for me, when I arrived for work."

Benji's gaze met mine, and I knew we were having the same exact thought.

We needed to see that security tape—we needed to see who had dropped off the bags. And how they had been able to access the vault without anyone seeing.

"WE'RE STARTING to get a good timeline," I said as Benji and I left the bank. "It was Jeremy who was in the show, but he never came back with the props or the costume. Peggy says she heard him ride through the clearing, so something happened between him riding through the old sets and arriving at the bank to return everything."

Benji nodded. "We also know that someone had

already taken the valuables from the safety deposit boxes when Claudia came in for work, because someone had filled the extra bags—so why hadn't anyone noticed?"

"Did you see how dead it was in there?" I said. "I doubt anyone even went into the vault until it was closing time and they were cleaning up."

Benji raised a shoulder. "Good point. But that was a big risk, leaving all the boxes for someone to find. What if someone had gone back there before the show? Kennedy would have discovered the missing items before Jeremy had ever had the chance to take them."

"People are trained to jump to conclusions and run with it. If I had been them, I'd assume that the valuables were long gone, not sitting in a cartoon bag, waiting to be stolen like it was every afternoon at four o'clock."

"Still, it was a big risk."

We stopped in front of the sheriff's station, and I glanced through the window. Deputy Steve was no longer at his usual spot.

"Think the sheriff will let us look at that tape?" Benji asked, noticing where my gaze had landed.

"Not a chance."

He glanced at me. "But if we can't look at the tape, we can't see who came in early and placed those bags."

Yeah, that was a problem.

"Even if we managed to get the tape, how would we watch it?" I asked. "It's on VHS. I bet the only place in this whole town that has a VHS player is...at the bank."

I spun to face Benji. "That's it. We need to find out if the sheriff's station has a VHS player. If not, then…"

"Then the sheriff never had any intention of watching the security footage," Benji finished for me. "If she had no way to watch the VHS tape, then she was likely trying to get rid of the evidence that implicated her brother."

I pumped a fist in the air. "Now we're on a roll."

And with all the confidence of someone who had no idea what they were doing but believed they did, I pushed the sheriff's station door open and marched in.

My grand entrance was wasted, however, when there was no one to watch it. Not only was the deputy not in his usual spot, he wasn't there at all, and neither was the sheriff.

There was, however, a bell on the counter.

I rang it a couple of times, then called, "Sheriff McKnight?"

The sheriff walked in from the back, looking both annoyed and amused. "You didn't even give me a chance to get up here. What's the emergency?"

"We need a VHS player," I said bluntly. "My mom stuck some old home videos in my suitcase for Benji and me to watch on our honeymoon—you know, 'remember the good old days and reminisce as you start this new journey together' kind of thing. But no one has a VHS player anymore. I wanted to ask Amy or Seth if they have one, but you have them both locked up here. Can I ask them where I can find one at the saloon?" I paused. "Actually, you wouldn't by any chance have one here, would you?"

Sheriff McKnight was quiet, and her hard stare pierced through me. "You came all the way here to ask me if I have a VHS player? I know that our sheriff's office might seem like a joke to you, but this is a functioning law enforcement office, not a hotel lobby. You can watch your tapes when you get back home." The sheriff then turned on her heel and disappeared into the back of the office.

That wasn't a no.

I was tempted to follow the sheriff, but Benji shook his head, already knowing what was going through my mind. He led me outside to the walkway, then turned to me. "We're already suspects, and us just being here is suspicious enough. And there is no way she believed that lie— who brings home videos on their honeymoon?"

"My mom," I said with no hesitation. It was absolutely believable that she would do something like that.

Benji's lips twitched up. "Unfortunately, Sheriff McKnight doesn't know your mom."

I frowned. "So, where does that leave us? We have no security tape, and Sheriff McKnight is anything but objective. Seth and Amy have been framed, but without proof, they are going to prison. It's hard to argue with evidence that is discovered at your place of business."

Benji quietly watched me, not answering right away.

"You believe they've been framed, don't you?" I asked.

"We don't know them, Maddie. I want to believe they

are innocent, but right now, not even we are in the clear. A murder weapon was found in our hotel room closet—never mind that we didn't know the guy and have no motive. And for someone to move a huge pile of rope and a horse and not look out of place? It would have to be someone who frequents the saloon and wouldn't raise suspicion if they were wandering about."

"I'm betting that everyone in this town visits the saloon," I said. "What else is there to do in a place like this?"

Benji looked frustrated as he raked his fingers through his hair. "Another question we need to ask ourselves is if the person who killed Jeremy is the same person who robbed the bank. The bags of valuables were already in place when Jeremy did the show, so either he has an accomplice or someone was using him. The teller could have placed the bags herself, but she doesn't have the combination to the vault, as far as we know. That leads us to the bank manager, Kennedy."

"I guess. But what about Sheriff McKnight?" I asked. "The station shares a wall with the bank, and her brother is literally the town's outlaw. It wouldn't have been difficult for them to work together. She could have stepped out long enough to steal the valuables and place the bags and get back before anyone noticed. I'm sure the sheriff is over there all the time, keeping an eye on things. Probably even has a key to the building. And now that the sheriff has the security tapes, no one can prove what happened—how much do you want to bet that she accidentally 'destroys' the tape?"

"It's possible," Benji said, "but I'm not sure I buy it. When I went out with the sheriff looking for evidence in the woods, she was beside herself, frantically scouring the ground, and every rock and tree trunk. I was the one who had to tell her there wasn't anything there." He paused. "Sheriff McKnight was devastated at the thought that her brother had been killed rather than skipped town like everyone was led to believe. Even though she insisted that Jeremy would never have stolen those valuables, she was hoping he had. Because then she wouldn't have to face a far bigger tragedy."

I thought of the small-statured sheriff with her fiery hair and personality to match. I had to agree with Benji. I had a hard time imagining her robbing a bank and then killing her brother.

"Okay, fine," I said. "It could have been Chuck, who tends to the landscaping all over town and would have easy access—everyone knows Chuck, and he works alongside the back entrances of both the sheriff's station and the bank."

"I could see it," Benji said. "We know he can be fiercely protective when he needs to be. And what about Phineas? He's apparently an influential member of the McKnight family. Getting rid of a problem like Jeremy, and pinning it on two of the most respected members of the Bloomfield family, would be a double win for the McKnights."

I frowned, thinking of all the possibilities. We didn't know this town well enough, or the people in it, to be investigating like this. There was too much history and family drama.

Over the past day, my headache had dissipated almost entirely, but now...it was back in full force. The stress was putting me over the edge.

"I don't have time for sneaking around or playing games," I said, spinning back toward the sheriff's station. "At this rate, we'll never figure out what happened to Jeremy, and we'll never know if Seth and Amy went to jail for something they didn't do. And then I'll have to pretend that none of it happened, because otherwise, it will keep me up at night, wondering what we missed—wondering what clue would have led us to the real killer."

Benji stepped between me and the sheriff's station, his forehead creased in worry. "What are you planning on doing?" He knew me well enough to know when I was about to do something crazy.

"What I should have done from the beginning—be direct and to the point. We're going to demand that the sheriff show us that video."

"If the sheriff really did want that video to help her discover who planted those bags, and there was incriminating evidence on it, she would already be on her way to make the arrest."

"Then we need to find out why she hasn't already done that." I paused. "No one in this town is presumed innocent —including the sheriff."

19

Benji didn't agree with my methods, but he wasn't able to come up with a better alternative, and so he stepped aside, allowing me to pass.

Once again, when I entered the sheriff's station, no one was at the desk.

"Shouldn't Deputy Steve be here or something?" I asked Benji. "He's always here."

Sheriff McKnight reappeared from the back, frowning. "He's on break." Her gaze jumped between Benji and me, and I noticed that my husband had opted to stay positioned by the door, like he was already planning his escape.

"I already told you I don't have a VHS player," she said, her voice filled with annoyance. "If you come in here again, I'm going to arrest you for being a public nuisance."

That was fair. Except, Sheriff McKnight had just

admitted what she's refused to earlier—that she didn't have a VHS player.

"If you don't have a VHS player, why did you take the security tape from the bank? You have nothing to play it on."

The sheriff looked at me like I'd lost my mind. "Why would I ask for the bank's security tape when I could just watch it there?" She raised an eyebrow. "Is this why you were pretending to have home videos you needed to watch? It was a stupid lie, by the way."

Benji had been right—she'd seen right through it. But I took offense at her calling it stupid. "You wouldn't be calling it stupid if you knew my mother," I started, but Sheriff McKnight cut me off.

"Why are you interested in the bank's security footage?" she asked, but then answered her own question. "Given your propensity to not leave things alone, I suppose you think you can do my job better than I can."

I didn't deny it. "Checking the bank's security cameras seems like one of the first things you'd want to do after a bank robbery."

"You're right, it is," the sheriff said, folding her arms across her chest and pinning me with her glare. She had been annoyed before—now she was getting mad.

I folded my arms and met her glare. "Why won't you let us help you?"

"For starters, I don't know you," Sheriff McKnight said. "More importantly, you are still suspects in Jeremy's disappearance, and I'd have to be crazy to trust you with something like this."

"Fine. Don't trust us. But why won't you hand the investigation over to someone else who isn't as emotionally tied to this case?" I asked. "I know what it's like for a case to be personal, and I wasn't at my best."

"Did you stop investigating?" the sheriff asked. "Did you hand it off to someone else so they could be *objective*?" She did air quotes around that last word.

I hesitated, and she knew exactly what that meant.

"The entire town thought it completely natural to believe my brother was a bank robber—no one batted an eye at the possibility," Sheriff McKnight spat out. "Now that it's likely that Jeremy did not rob the bank and instead was murdered, do you think anyone is coming by with their apologies? Anyone saying they'd known he'd never do such a thing? Of course not. Because he was Jeremy. Now they're saying they always knew he'd lead a short life —I'm the only one in this town who seems to want to figure out what actually happened to him."

"Amy wants to figure it out—she was in love with him, despite his flaws," I said. "But you locked up the one person who would help you."

"And what choice did I have?" Sheriff McKnight said, throwing her arms in the air. "His horse and the missing noose were found in the saloon—in your closet." She paused, then leaned on the counter, getting close. "This is not the honeymoon that either of you wanted, and it's not going to get any better. I've changed my mind about you two staying—I want you both to leave. Now."

The sheriff, as usual, was trying to get rid of us. But I wouldn't be swayed so easily.

"Jeremy is missing—most likely murdered—and we can help you discover who did it," I said, placing my hands on the counter and meeting her gaze.

Sheriff McKnight took a step back, a brief flash of surprise crossing her face. "This is none of your business." She paused. "I'm giving you an out. Why don't you want to take it?"

That was a good question.

"Because she has an insatiable desire to help people," Benji said, stepping forward. "It doesn't matter that we've only been here a couple of days. Maddie doesn't know how to do anything less than her best to keep innocent people out of jail."

Sheriff McKnight was quiet for a moment. "You're very sure of Seth's and Amy's innocence. Are you implying that you have a lead on who is actually responsible for Jeremy's disappearance?"

I shook my head. "We don't have enough information. The horse and the noose don't prove anything—they're likely just a distraction from what's really going on. I was hoping the security tape would help."

Sheriff McKnight seemed relieved by my answer. "Like I said, I don't have the security tape. I did request to watch it, but Kennedy said it would need to wait—it wasn't a good time."

"If you requested to watch the tape—" I started, but the sheriff cut me off.

"No more. You are going to go back to the hotel, pack your bags, and find a different honeymooning spot."

The sheriff's gaze bore into me, and I wasn't about to argue with all five feet of her. She wasn't going to give me any more information than she already had.

"Fine," I said. "But if someone in your town killed Jeremy and you pin it on Amy and Seth because it was the easy answer, that will be on you."

And then I stormed out of the office.

Once outside on the walkway, I waited for Benji to catch up.

"That was quite the exit," he said, joining me.

"Thank you."

"We're not leaving, though, are we."

It was a statement, not a question. He knew we weren't going anywhere.

"Of course not," I said. "We're going to the bank to talk to Kennedy and find out why the sheriff was never allowed to watch that security tape."

Benji sighed. "Look, Maddie, you know I want to figure out who killed Jeremy as much as you do. We saw his body —his face. We were led to believe that we were crazy— when we clearly weren't. But the sheriff wasn't kidding around when she told us to leave town. Do you really want us to add being arrested to the crazy things we've done on this honeymoon?"

"We aren't going to be arrested," I said, turning toward the bank. "I need to stop by the bank to see if they have an ATM machine. The sheriff can't arrest me for that."

"You don't even have an account with the bank," Benji said, but he knew better than to try to stop me, so he followed me next door.

"Claudia," I said as I walked through the front door. "We're back."

The teller smiled. "Did you forget something while you were in here?"

I nodded. "I did, actually. But it's a bit sensitive. Would it be possible for me to speak with Kennedy?"

"Sure. Let me just make sure he's not busy."

Claudia opened a door in the barred counter and walked to the back of the bank.

"There really isn't much security," I said, eyeing the open door. I could easily walk back there while she was distracted and help myself to whatever cash happened to be sitting loose.

The teller returned shortly and gestured for us to follow her. "Kennedy is quite busy today, but he says he has a few minutes to speak with you."

"Thank you," I told her, before following her into the back of the bank. Rather than a fancy office, like most bank managers would have, it seemed that Kennedy's office doubled as the security room with a small TV set up, showing him what was going on in the lobby.

Kennedy was an older man with long white hair and an accompanying mustache. He sat behind a desk that looked like it had been picked up from a thrift store, and his chair had certainly seen better days. It looked like managing a bank in Dusty Ridge wasn't as lucrative as one would expect, and I was sure that Kennedy wouldn't mind a fifty-thousand-dollar bonus to help set him up for retirement.

"Hi, Kennedy. My name is Maddison Swallows, and this is my husband, Benji," I said, extending a hand.

Kennedy glanced at it but didn't move to take it. "Yes, I know who you are."

Of course he did.

"We are just stopping by because the sheriff mentioned that she had asked to see the security tape a couple of days ago, but that you had mentioned it wasn't a good time. Is now a better time for her to come see what's on that tape?"

"Sheriff McKnight did not send you here," Kennedy said, his gaze cool. "Tess doesn't trust easily, let alone two tourists who both claim to have found her brother's body, only to lose it fifteen minutes later."

"That's not a fair representation of what happened—" I started, but Kennedy cut me off with a wave of his hand.

"That begs the question of why you are really here," the bank manager said. "It's likely because there is something on that video that you do not want me to see—like who really broke into my vault."

"Why wouldn't we want you to see the one thing that can clear both our names, as well as Seth's and Amy's?" Benji asked. "Don't you want to know who is responsible?"

"I already know who was responsible," Kennedy said, leaning back in his chair and placing his hands over his stomach.

I raised an eyebrow. "Then why haven't you shared your information with the sheriff?"

"I have. Jeremy broke into the vault, thinking that the safety deposit keys that Chuck stole would still work. When they didn't, he went with plan B and drilled into the boxes, stealing fifty-thousand dollars' worth of valuables— it's as simple as that."

I shared a confused look with Benji. "You're saying that you saw him steal the items, then plant the bags, on the video? Chuck said that he never stole the keys to the safety deposit boxes—that you only told people you'd fired him because he'd asked you to."

"Chuck has had a difficult life, and his job at the bank was just one in a string of many—he never stays in one place too long," Kennedy said. "And let's be honest, the keys went missing for two days and then someone mysteriously turned them in at the sheriff's station? Chuck had the easiest access to them; it only makes sense that he stole the keys and made copies during that time. He and Jeremy were probably planning the theft all this time."

It sounded simple—and logical.

"You sound like you're guessing—that you didn't see him actually do it," I pressed. "Surely insurance won't pay out without proof of who stole it—they could easily think you had staged it."

I knew I was going into dangerous territory: indirectly accusing the bank manager of robbing his own bank.

But it worked.

Kennedy sat up in his chair, his lips pursed and his eyes narrow. "Safety deposit boxes are uninsurable, which means that I have members of this town calling me, stopping by the bank—threatening me—if I don't find their jewels and prized possessions. Trust me when I say that I did not rob my own bank, and I certainly am not purposely keeping that security tape from the sheriff."

"Then why won't you show her the video?" Benji asked. "If you would just—"

Kennedy's expression tightened, and he stood from his desk before yelling, "Because the security tape is missing. Stolen. Just like everything else. Happy?"

20

No, I wasn't happy. Not happy at all.

"Why wouldn't you tell the sheriff that?" I asked. "That's kind of a big deal."

Kennedy pulled at his mustache, his gaze boring into us. "What would I tell her, exactly? That the only evidence showing that I did not rob my own bank had suspiciously gone missing?"

A knock on the door behind us caused Kennedy's gaze to snap up, and he barked, "Come in."

Claudia poked her head in, looking embarrassed. "I'm sorry, I didn't mean to eavesdrop, but you were yelling kind of loud and—"

Kennedy released a long sigh and slumped into the chair at his desk. "What is it, Claudia?"

"I'm sorry if I caused any trouble, but when Sheriff McKnight requested to watch the video, I assumed she wanted to watch it over at the station, so I ran it next door for her."

Kennedy straightened. "You what?"

Claudia looked close to tears, like she was afraid she'd done something wrong, and she gave a small nod. "I'm sorry. I thought you knew. I didn't realize she'd never received it."

I wasn't so sure that she hadn't.

"We should get out of your hair," I said, standing from my chair. Benji followed suit. "We do appreciate your help, though, and—"

Kennedy raised a shaky finger at us, and it looked like we might be in for a lecture, but then he spoke in a quiet voice. "Please don't mention this to anyone. It's something that needs to be taken care of in-house. If Sheriff McKnight is covering something up—"

"Then you want to be the one to confront her," I finished for him. "Got it."

"I'm not saying she's the one who did it," Kennedy said. "She might not have been the one to break into the vault— she doesn't have the combination code. But she does have a key to the building." He seemed to be talking more to himself than us. It was like he was trying to convince himself that the sheriff wasn't capable of doing something like that.

Benji and I turned to leave Kennedy with his thoughts, but then I turned back. "Kennedy, I'm sorry, I have just one more question. Does everyone in town know that you have a security camera in here?"

"Probably. I've had it for decades."

I gave a thoughtful nod. "Thank you for your time. I know you are a busy man." And then Benji and I left Claudia and Kennedy.

"Why would someone break into the vault and rob it if they knew they'd be on camera?" I asked Benji once we were outside.

"Maybe they forgot. It's like you put up a picture in your house and then you get so used to walking by it every day that you stop remembering it's there. Someone could take the picture off the wall, and you wouldn't notice because it's become invisible."

That was generally true—for those not planning on robbing a bank and killing the fall guy. I wasn't so sure it applied to this situation. Surely you'd remember there was a security camera.

We started walking back toward the saloon, but I remembered that we hadn't eaten lunch and the restaurant would be closed without Seth and Amy there. The thought made me sad.

"I noticed when we signed up for the ghost town tour that the hotel had a restaurant," I said. "Want to get dinner and then see if they have any rooms available?" We weren't allowed back in the saloon now that the owners were in jail and our hotel room had become a crime scene. Thankfully, the sheriff had at least allowed us to pack up our bags—after they'd gone through all of our belongings to make sure we weren't harboring any other evidence.

Benji eyed me, like he thought I was up to something, but ultimately agreed. "All right. There is another restaurant down the street—" he started, but I cut him off.

"No, the hotel will be fine."

He gave me another curious look but then turned at the fire station. "The hotel it is."

I wasn't up to something—not really. But something was still bugging me, and as we walked, I couldn't stop thinking about it.

If someone knew they would be on camera while they were robbing a bank, it seemed they'd either need to wear a disguise, or they really had forgotten that it was there, until it was too late.

Hence the need to steal the security tape.

It wouldn't have been difficult for someone to set Jeremy up by wearing his costume when breaking into the vault and planting the bags of money. They would have wanted Kennedy to watch the video—they would have wanted him to make assumptions about who was behind the mask.

Sheriff McKnight would have had access to her brother's costume, but if it had been her who had stolen the valuables, she wouldn't have taken the security tape and then lied about not having it. She'd want people to see it.

"Could they really have forgotten about it?" I mused.

"What?" Benji asked, glancing at me, and I was unsure if he hadn't heard me or if he thought he'd heard wrong.

We took a left turn, and the hotel came into view. And so did the green door.

"Kennedy thinks that Chuck could have made copies of the safety deposit keys," I said. "And who does Chuck have a weird friendship with?"

Benji's gaze jumped to the green door. "You can't be serious. After everything Amy told us, you want to go back?"

"He could be the one who set Jeremy up. He wouldn't have fit into Jeremy's costume of course, but didn't Amy say that Jeremy used to work for Phineas? And Kennedy mentioned that the sheriff is the only other person who has a key to the building. It all makes sense—Chuck copies the safety deposit keys, Jeremy takes his sister's key to the building, goes in and steals the valuables, and Phineas uses his influence to keep anyone from getting too close. They make a deal to split it all evenly, and everyone goes home happy."

"You're saying that you think all three of them were in on it."

I nodded. "Yes."

"And you think that Phineas was the one who killed Jeremy and then covered it up. Even though they likely had been working together."

I hesitated to respond, because I knew what Benji was getting at—if Phineas had hanged Jeremy, why would we knowingly go back into that basement without any support from law enforcement?

"I don't know," I finally answered.

Benji shook his head. "I don't think this is a good idea, Maddie. If this was planned a long time ago, then that means our original assumption that grabbing the noose was a spur of the moment decision, is wrong. I'd really just like to get dinner, go on our tour tomorrow morning, and then take the sheriff's advice. We need to leave."

Benji was right. Of course he was. But I could tell the answer was right in front of us—one more conversation might be all that was needed to tip the scales and give us the answers we were looking for.

I raised a finger. "I only have one question for Phineas. And I'll stay outside on the steps in the wide open where everyone can see." Before Benji could stop me, I hurried past him, taking the steps two at a time.

Phineas had been watching, and, once again, he opened the door before I had the chance to knock.

"I thought you would have left town by now," he said, leaning against the door frame. "Since you don't have a place to stay."

"Yes, you'd think that," I said. "We're going to see if the hotel here has any availability, and then we'll be leaving tomorrow afternoon. But I do have one question for you, before we go."

Phineas stayed silent. I took that as permission to speak.

"Why Chuck?"

Phineas tilted his head to the side. "I don't know what you mean."

"Why are you friends with Chuck?" I clarified. "You two couldn't be more different, and yet he thinks the world of you. He pranks you because he craves your attention—your friendship. I'm wondering if it goes both ways."

Phineas smirked. "Chuck and me go way back, long before I ever left for LA. He doesn't prank me because he craves my attention—he pranks me because he's trying to even the score from when we were young. And every time he's successful, he makes sure I know it."

"So, it isn't a friendship—it's a rivalry?" I asked.

Phineas shook his head. "There aren't many people in this town that I trust, but I would trust Chuck with my life." He paused and glanced up to the top of the staircase, where Benji was waiting for me, his phone pulled out, just in case he needed to call the sheriff.

"But if you trust Chuck—" I started.

Phineas cut me off. "You said you had one question, and I answered two. Safe travels tomorrow." And then he shut the door in my face.

"Did you get what you needed?" Benji asked when I rejoined him at the top of the stairs.

I nodded slowly. "I think I did. Let's get dinner."

Benji studied me as we walked, like he was trying to guess what was on my mind.

"Did you figure out something?" he asked.

"I have a hunch, but it will take some doing to prove it right."

Benji frowned. "Does proving it mean putting yourself in danger?"

I hesitated, and I could tell that Benji didn't appreciate me not being able to answer right away.

"I won't be in danger," I said. "Probably. I'll make sure Sheriff McKnight is there, as well as Deputy Steve."

That didn't seem to do much to assuage Benji's concerns, considering that the sheriff herself was still one of our top suspects; however, he took my hand and gave it a squeeze.

"If we can help Seth and Amy before we leave, then we need to do it," Benji finally said. "But I really do need to eat first."

"Agreed. We can't go accusing people of things they may or may not have done on an empty stomach."

And then we went into the hotel and had the best chicken pot pie I'd ever had in my entire life.

I just hoped we'd be able to get everyone in the same place on such short notice.

21

B enji and I walked into the sheriff's office, and Deputy Steve did not look pleased to see us.

"You can't be here," he whispered. "The sheriff ordered me to arrest you if you came back."

"We're very aware," I said. "But we need to speak with her—she'll want to hear what we have to say."

The deputy's lips pursed in skepticism. "I highly doubt that."

I reached out and hit the bell that sat on the counter. "I'm willing to take the risk."

The deputy grumbled, but he walked into the back of the station, presumably to let her know we were requesting her presence.

"What's the plan?" Benji asked, his voice low.

"It's in the works, but I'll keep you updated as we go along."

He blinked. "So, you still have no idea who is actually behind Jeremy's death? What if it's the sheriff?"

"It isn't," Sheriff McKnight said, entering from the back. "I thought I told you to leave town." She glanced over her shoulder. "And I thought I told Deputy Steve to arrest you," she called.

No answer from the back.

"He's ignoring me," she said.

I smiled. "You did, but don't be mad at the deputy. It's not his fault we don't listen."

The sheriff harrumphed. "What are you doing here?"

"We know what happened to Jeremy, and we need your help proving it," I said with all the confidence in the world. Never mind that I only had suspicions, nothing concrete, and I was hoping that a couple of key players would break as easily as I thought they would.

The sheriff narrowed her eyes and crossed her arms over her chest. "Tell me one good reason why I should play along with your little Nancy Drew fantasy."

"Because you want to know what happened to your brother, and you want to see justice served, regardless of what it looks like." When the sheriff still didn't look convinced, I added, "And because you want to be rid of us."

Sheriff McKnight raised an eyebrow, like it was now worth considering, but she remained silent for several long seconds. "I need more than that. Do you have proof?"

"Sure I do. At the museum. And I have a list of people that you need to make sure show up for it."

I could tell that Sheriff McKnight really didn't want to entertain the idea that I might actually be helpful, but I knew the moment her curiosity won out, because she sighed and held out a hand to me.

"Give me the list."

I tried not to look too pleased when I gave her the names, but it was really hard not to.

"Think you can have everyone there in an hour?" I asked.

The sheriff glanced over the names. "The sooner, the better."

I POSITIONED the last chair next to the empty case that used to house the stolen noose, and then looked over my handywork. Nine chairs were placed neatly in a circle. Benji and I wouldn't be sitting, so we didn't need chairs for us. That left chairs for the sheriff, Deputy Steve, Peggy, Seth, Amy, Phineas, Chuck, Kennedy, and Claudia.

"That's a lot of potential suspects," Benji said. "You sure you know what you're doing? It seems premature."

Of course I didn't know what I was doing. But whether we solved this or not, Benji and I would be leaving town the next day, and Seth and Amy would be on their own. I needed to at least try.

I was saved from answering when Sheriff McKnight walked in, followed by the deputy, Peggy, Seth, and Amy.

Peggy was messing with Seth's hair, chastising the sheriff for not taking better care of him.

"He hasn't even been in there overnight," Sheriff McKnight said, sounding impatient, like this wasn't the first time she'd been on the receiving end of Peggy's criticism.

"Where is everyone else?" I asked, worried that they wouldn't show up.

"They'll be here," the sheriff said, gesturing for the others to take a seat.

"You too, sheriff," I said.

She glanced at me, surprise etched in her features. "You can't be serious."

"Please."

The sheriff must not have realized that I still considered her a suspect, and she looked like she might leave the room, but Phineas and Chuck arrived at that moment, with Kennedy and Claudia not far behind.

"I prefer to stand," she said. "Law enforcement needs to always be at the ready."

Deputy Steve looked between the seats and the sheriff, seemingly trying to figure out if he should also stand. Sheriff McKnight solved the problem by directing him to take a position on the opposite side of the circle, and he seemed more than happy to oblige.

"I guess that leaves two seats for you and your husband," the sheriff said, nodding toward the chairs.

I supposed that did.

I took a seat next to Chuck, with Benji on my other side next to Peggy.

"What is this all about, Sheriff?" Kennedy asked. "You made it sound urgent." Judging by the limited interactions I'd had with him, the bank manager was never pleasant, but he was even less so this evening.

"You've all been invited here because of previous interactions you've had with Jeremy," the sheriff said. "He wasn't exactly popular in town, but that didn't mean he deserved to die. So, we're going to sit down and figure things out once and for all—who killed my brother?"

Phineas immediately jumped to his feet, announcing that he wasn't going to put up with it, and Kennedy quickly joined him.

"Sit down," the sheriff barked. "Think of it more as a group therapy session." And then she nodded to me.

Group therapy was exactly what this looked like—and what it would likely turn into.

Phineas and Kennedy both glared in my direction, but they followed the sheriff's orders and sat down.

"Kennedy and Claudia," I began. "You saw Jeremy every day at the bank when he would rob you for the show, and then again when Jeremy would return the props and the dirty costume, exchanging it for a clean one." My gaze moved to their right. "Phineas, Jeremy used to work for you, before he was fired. I'm not clear on why he was let go, but we'll circle back to that in a minute."

I then looked at Seth and Amy. "Amy, you were in love

with Jeremy, despite his flaws, and Seth, you hated that she stayed with him after the way he'd treated her all these years." Seth opened his mouth in protest, but I held up a finger, letting him know I wasn't finished, as my gaze moved to Chuck. "Chuck, you knew Jeremy in the same way you know everyone in town. You're the one who likes everyone, and who everyone likes in return."

Chuck beamed at the compliment and nodded. "I hate to brag, but it's true."

"People tell you things—they probably also talk around you, not worried if you overhear, because they know you won't tell anyone. They trust you."

I highly doubted this was true—Chuck was likely the sole reason that gossip travelled so quickly through town, but Chuck didn't refute the claim, and instead smiled and nodded.

"That makes me think that you know a lot more about Jeremy's disappearance than you're letting on," I said.

Chuck's smile immediately vanished. He opened his mouth to speak, but no words came out.

"It's all right," I said. "You're safe here, remember? These are your friends, and you have the sheriff and her deputy here."

Chuck's nervous gaze bounced around the circle, but it landed on two people in particular.

Good, that helped me know who to focus on.

"I don't know anything about what happened to Jeremy," Chuck said. He looked at the sheriff. "Honest."

I gave him another reassuring smile. "I believe you."

"You do?" he said, obviously surprised.

"Yes, I do. But I also think that you really did copy the safety deposit keys—it wasn't just a rumor so you would appear tough. You were involved in the bank robbery."

"I didn't copy them," he insisted.

"If you didn't, then you allowed someone else to."

Chuck looked like he wanted to melt into his seat, and this time, he remained silent.

That was one piece of the puzzle taken care of. Only ninety-nine left to go.

My gaze landed on Claudia. "Jeremy came in as usual for the show. You knew it was him because of his unique mannerisms. Nothing appeared amiss when he left."

"That's correct," she said, fidgeting with the end of her long-sleeve blouse.

"Jeremy always took the same route when he left town during the show," I said, my gaze circling. "He'd leave down the road, then circle back through the woods, where he'd change out of his costume and then cut through the old movie sets so he could return the props and costume. Except, he didn't change this time."

"How could you possibly know that?" Phineas asked, looking annoyed.

"Because Jeremy never left the woods, evidenced by my husband and me finding his body in those woods a couple hours after the show."

Peggy raised her hand. "There is no proof that you

found his body. I heard him ride past the museum, like he always does. I caught a glimpse of him jumping the fence and racing through the old movie sets."

"How many people know Jeremy's routine after the show?" I asked her. "Could someone else, posing as him, ride past so that no one would know that something was amiss?"

She paused, seeming surprised by the question, like it had never occurred to her. "I suppose they could have. All of us along that strip of Main Street see him racing behind our stores each day."

"So, you're saying that he races past the museum and the sheriff's office in order to get to the bank, where he returns the costume and props."

Peggy nodded. "Yeah."

My gaze moved to Kennedy and Claudia. "You said that he didn't return the props and costume that day."

"He didn't," Claudia insisted.

"So, either Peggy needs to get her eyesight checked, or the person who was posing as Jeremy rode to a different location."

"My eyes are fine," Peggy grumbled. "Twenty-twenty and never needed glasses."

"So, we don't know where our imposter rode to, but we do know that the horse ultimately ended up in the saloon stable." I turned to Seth and Amy, because I couldn't appear to have favorites. "Deputy Steve found Jeremy's horse in your stable and the missing noose in your upstairs closet."

"You mean in the closet where you two were staying," Phineas piped up.

I nodded, conceding his point. "Yes, it's true. I suppose my husband and I shouldn't be counted out as suspects either." I turned back to Seth and Amy. "What do you normally keep in your stable back there?"

"Jeremy's horse," Amy said. "He needed a place to keep Bullet, and I didn't mind letting him use it."

"You didn't just let him use it," Seth complained. "You ended up being the person to feed and water the horse, groom it, muck out the stall—"

"If you didn't know that Bullet was back in the stable," I interrupted, "who has been taking care of the horse since Jeremy's death?"

Amy raised a shoulder. "There would have already been food and water in the stable from that morning, and the deputy found the horse the next day. He wouldn't have gone without food for long."

That brought me to the noose.

And this was the crux of it.

"Okay, so whoever returned Bullet wanted to make sure that he was well taken care of, even risking returning the horse to his stable. Of course, our imposter was wearing the costume, so it wasn't all that big of a risk," I said. "The noose, though—that's different. When my husband and I checked in, you said that we were the only ones with access to the elevator that would take us upstairs."

"That's the truth," Seth said. "Other than Amy and me, you two would be the only ones with keycards. We value privacy at our establishment." Seth didn't realize the implication of his statement until after he'd already said it, and his eyes widened. "Not that Amy or I had anything to do with Jeremy's disappearance, or the noose. And not that I'm implying that you did either."

"I understand," I said, smiling so he knew there were no hard feelings. "What I'm curious about is how Deputy Steve was able to go to the suite without a keycard. He was the one who miraculously found the noose, after all."

All eyes turned on the deputy.

22

The deputy's face paled. "I-I'm law enforcement," he stuttered. "I'm allowed."

"No one said you weren't allowed," I said. "But I was there with Amy when the sheriff arrived, and I never saw you until you walked from the elevator with an armful of rope. How did you get up there?"

"There is a set of stairs," he said, his gaze landing on the sheriff, pleading with her to back him up. "It is required to have more than one way to enter and exit the second floor, in case of emergency. But access to go up the stairs requires a security code that only a few people know."

"You and the sheriff are among them."

The deputy nodded. "For safety reasons."

I was starting to doubt my hypothesis, but then I saw the deputy's gaze land on Phineas, who was staring straight ahead, making a point of not turning around as Deputy Steve spoke. Everyone else did, though.

I pressed on.

"Here is what I propose," I said. "I don't know what happened between the time that Jeremy disappeared and Benji and I found him." I turned my gaze on Phineas. "But I think that whoever killed Jeremy was his partner in crime. They had planned to meet up in the woods, and Jeremy would transfer the valuables to his accomplice, who would hide them away until they could sell them. But Jeremy's partner got greedy and killed him."

Phineas tilted his head with a curious gaze, his lips twitching up at the corners, as if I amused him.

"Your theory is preposterous," the sheriff interrupted. "Jeremy stumbled upon someone else's plan, and they killed him for it. It's the only logical explanation."

The sheriff was willing to believe anything except that her brother was guilty.

Not surprisingly, Amy added, "I agree with the sheriff. Jeremy had been working to turn his life around, and he'd never been a thief."

I was tempted to discount their blind loyalty to Jeremy —but then I realized they could be right. It would be easy enough for someone to place the bags at the bank without Jeremy knowing what was in them. He had been requesting additional bags for months to add to the realism of the show, and he may have merely thought that people had listened.

"If you want to prove that Jeremy didn't know he was helping rob the bank, we need to turn our attention to who had access to the security code at the saloon, as well as who had the combination code for the vault."

My gaze landed on Kennedy, and he raised his arms in a defensive position. "Don't look at me. I came in late that day because my cat was sick."

I moved my gaze to Claudia, who looked like she was near tears. "I don't have access to the vault. Like I told you before, Kennedy doesn't trust anyone else with that kind of thing."

"He used to," I said. I looked at Chuck. "You didn't ask Kennedy to fire you—he *did* fire you. Because the keys really did go missing for two days. That was plenty of time for you to make copies, then anonymously drop them off at the sheriff's station, as if they'd been lost. You work all over town, trimming and mowing—making sure the town looks beautiful for its guests. It wouldn't have been hard. And I'd bet you knew the combination to the vault as well."

Chuck's expression became panicked, and his gaze jumped to Phineas—just as the deputy's had. "I swear I didn't steal those keys—I lost them. Even though they showed up a couple days later at the sheriff's station, Kennedy wouldn't believe me."

"What is your relationship with Phineas?" I asked him, abruptly changing the subject. My intention had been to catch him off guard, and it worked.

Chuck's lips parted. "What?"

"When I accused you of copying the keys, you looked at Phineas, as if wondering how to answer. Why?"

Sheriff McKnight could see how uncomfortable I had made Chuck, and she stepped forward. "Maddison, you're scaring the poor man." She glanced at Chuck, who looked like he was about to throw up, and she shook her head. "I never should have agreed to gather everyone like this. You are doing nothing more than throwing around baseless accusations, hoping to find something that sticks."

The sheriff was partially correct—I was fishing. But my accusations weren't baseless.

"Phineas told me he works alone," I said.

"And that's true," Phineas said.

I held up a finger, letting him know that I wasn't finished. "Why did you hire Jeremy if you work alone?"

"It was more like an internship," Phineas said. "He wanted to learn some real skills that he could use to get ahead in the world, and an internship at the shop that makes the Grammys would give him a real leg up in the world. We worked together for about a year, but then he started showing up to the shop drunk. I work in a dangerous environment where people could get really hurt. I fired him, and I haven't worked with anyone since."

"And yet, there was someone in your shop the day we were there. Someone in the back who was trying to remain unseen." I paused. "Your shop seems like an easy place to hide a couple of bags of jewels. It's not the cleanest place in the world—it's not meant to be. You also don't have people coming and going, so there isn't much risk of being found out. That, and people are scared of you. I've noticed that you carry a lot of weight in this town."

Phineas's eyes narrowed, but he remained silent, as did the rest of the room. It was as if no one dared to breathe.

"Sheriff McKnight, would you be willing to test my theory and look for the valuables in Phineas's shop?" I asked, glancing at her.

For the first time since we'd started this pow-wow, the sheriff looked like she actually agreed with me. Without missing a beat, she said, "It doesn't hurt to take a look, unless Phineas has a reason why I shouldn't."

"I can go look while you finish questioning people," Deputy Steve offered, already starting for the door.

"I actually need the deputy to stay," I said. "There's something I need his help with."

Sheriff McKnight hesitated but nodded. "All right."

"But—" the deputy started.

She held up a hand. "I'm going to go search the shop. You stay."

The sheriff didn't even have time to leave the room before Phineas unraveled.

"I had nothing to do with it, only agreed to let him use my shop to store the bags in return for a percentage of the profits," Phineas blurted out. "I swear I didn't have anything to do with their theft, and certainly nothing to do with Jeremy's death. He'll tell you otherwise, but it's not true. It was all him."

And there it was.

"Chuck?" Sheriff McKnight said, turning to the groundskeeper, looking stunned. "You did this?"

Chuck looked like he was going to burst into tears, so I stepped in.

"No, not Chuck. I believe that he really did lose those keys, and if you'll remember, they were turned in to the sheriff's station. That's when Jeremy's killer first saw his opportunity."

Sheriff McKnight looked at me, bewildered.

"There is one other person who manages to be everywhere, all the time," I continued. "Someone who can come and go as they please, without raising suspicion."

My gaze settled on Deputy Steve. "The sheriff's office shares a wall with the bank—you knew Jeremy's entire schedule. You were also directly involved with the investigation and had access to all information in real time. You were there when Benji and I first reported the dead body. You were there when I came in, looking for Benji and the sheriff, when they'd gone out looking for clues, and your suggestion to me was to go back to the hotel room to get some rest. You were the one to find the noose in the upstairs closet at the saloon—almost like you knew exactly where it would be. You were the one to discover Jeremy's horse was back in the stable. And you were the one that

Claudia gave the security tape to at the office—you're probably also the one who requested it."

"It's all circumstantial," the deputy said, though he looked positively scared. This was not a man who was used to breaking the law, or being interrogated.

"I'm not finished yet," I said, but was interrupted when Phineas leapt to his feet.

"I'm not going down for grand larceny and murder," he shouted, turning to face the deputy for the first time since he'd sat down. "I didn't sign up for any of it."

The deputy remained silent, knowing that any attempt at rebuttal would likely incriminate himself.

Phineas turned his gaze on the sheriff. "Yes, you'll find the valuables in the back of the shop. They are no longer in the bank bags but are scattered throughout a few boxes of tools back there. The deputy was the one who planted the bags for Jeremy to take from the bank—Jeremy had no idea what was in them. The deputy had been asked to unlock the back door of the bank for Claudia that morning, because Kennedy was going to be late. He purposely arrived twenty minutes early and was able to open the vault with the combination that he'd found attached to the security deposit keys a year earlier—Chuck had written it down, because he was always forgetting it. I swear to you that I hadn't realized that Steve's plan was to intercept Jeremy when he circled back through the woods, or that Steve planned to knock Jeremy out and steal the bags."

"So, what went wrong?" I asked, considering that Jeremy hadn't merely been knocked unconscious.

"Steve hit Jeremy too hard," the sheriff surmised, and she looked at the deputy as if she were seeing him for the very first time.

His eyes widened in fear when he realized the sheriff believed Phineas.

The deputy turned to run, but the sheriff tackled him before he had the chance. She whipped out her handcuffs, slapped them onto the deputy's wrists, and held him on the ground.

"Tell us the rest," she said to Phineas as she tried to catch her breath.

Phineas hesitated but then continued. "Jeremy was supposed to be the fall guy that everyone believed robbed the bank, but after Steve realized he had accidentally killed Jeremy, he rode Jeremy's horse past the museum, then around to me, panicked. I suppose I have had a bit of a reputation in town of being rough around the edges— not always being on the up and up. I told Steve I would help him fix things for a percentage of the profits after he sold what he'd stolen." He paused. "I'm not proud of what I did, and I'll accept any punishment you see fit."

The sheriff didn't give any indication what that might be, and she waved a hand, asking him to continue.

"I'm guessing that Steve wasn't strong enough to move the body," I said.

"He wasn't," Phineas confirmed. "He also doesn't have

the stomach for it—threw up several times just talking about what happened. Besides, it was only a matter of time before someone would find Jeremy. We needed to act quickly." He glanced at Steve, handcuffed on the ground, as if ensuring he was still secure. "I had nowhere to take the body without someone seeing, so I decided to stage the body so it looked like he killed himself. I snuck into the museum when I knew that Peggy and Seth would be preoccupied and grabbed the noose."

Peggy and Seth shared alarmed looks at the realization that it had been stolen while they had both been in the museum.

"Maybe we should keep our social calls to the evening hours from now on," Peggy whispered.

"I'm good with that," Seth agreed.

The sheriff ignored the pair, her sole focus on Phineas. "Did you really think people would believe that Jeremy committed suicide?" Her voice was cold. "That wasn't the Jeremy that people knew—he wasn't a quitter, even when he should have."

Phineas gave a helpless shrug. "No, I didn't. Especially with the gash on his head. I hoped that people would think he hurt himself while trying to get the rope around the tree, or maybe while climbing it. My other idea was to make it seem like the horse had thrown him, but no one was going to believe that either—Bullet was fearless, and Jeremy shared a bond with that horse that no one else did."

I raised my hand, and Phineas's lips twitched up at the corners as he glanced my way. "Yes?"

"I don't understand why you didn't just bury the body out there in the woods and make people think he really had left town with all that jewelry."

Red tinged Phineas's cheeks. "We couldn't find his phone," he said, obviously embarrassed by the admission. "We didn't know if it had dropped when he had jumped off Bullet, ready to change out of his costume, or if it was back at the bank. If his phone could be traced to where he was buried, it would be game over for both of us."

I glanced at the sheriff. "Did you ever find it?"

Sheriff McKnight's lips tightened in a grim smile. "Yes —he always left it at home before a show. Never took it with him."

Steve tried throwing the sheriff off his back as he flung his body toward Phineas. "You stupid man. I can't believe you went through all that effort, and he never even had it on him."

"I guess there's only two questions left, then," Benji said, trying to speak over Steve's yells. "You went to the trouble of hanging Jeremy from the tree, hoping people would be stupid enough to think he committed suicide— why did you cut him back down, and where is he now?"

We all looked at Phineas, but for once, he didn't seem to have the answers. "I don't know—it wasn't me."

Our gazes swiveled to Steve.

"Well?" Sheriff McKnight said, lightly kicking Steve

with the toe of her boot. It hadn't looked hard, but he yelped in pain.

"How am I supposed to know? I didn't touch him."

"You mean, except when you killed him," Amy said, her voice shaking with anger.

My gaze landed on the only person in the circle who no longer looked interested in what was going on—Chuck was picking dirt out of his fingernails, looking like he was going to be sick.

"Chuck?" I asked him. "Where is Jeremy?"

His gaze shot up, and he looked startled at being addressed. "I don't—" he started, but it wasn't believable in the slightest.

"Yes, you do."

Chuck threw a panicked look at the sheriff, then released a resigned sigh. "Fine. When I was cleaning up from work, I saw Phineas hang Jeremy up in the trees."

"And you thought he'd killed him."

Chuck nodded. "Whatever reason he'd done it, I was sure that it was a good one—everyone knew what Jeremy was like—and I didn't want Phineas getting into any trouble."

"So, you cut down Jeremy and hid the body so it wouldn't be traced back to Phineas."

Chuck gave another nod.

Phineas groaned. "Why would you do that? You could have been seen, and then you'd be the one in trouble."

Chuck raised a shoulder. "Because we're friends, and

you'd do the same for me. Even with Jeremy's epiphany on wanting to be a better person, I couldn't let you be punished for something that everyone else in town has fantasized about. The museum had just closed, and after I sent those two away to find your shop," he nodded to me and Benji, "I knew I had some time. Besides, it would give you an alibi if they could say they'd been with you. They didn't go, of course, so that didn't do you any good."

Phineas's gaze softened. "I appreciate the gesture, Chuck, but you can't do stuff like that. Even for your friends."

Sheriff McKnight cleared her throat. "Not to interrupt this touching moment, but where is my brother now?"

"I'm guessing he's right here," I said, looking around the museum. "Chuck wouldn't have been able to take Jeremy far, especially on his own."

Chuck looked surprised that I'd figured it out. "In the large freezer behind the museum that they use for special events," he said. "Take out the key lime pies, and you'll find him."

Peggy looked like she might gag. "Guess I'm going to have to throw those out."

"I'd still eat them," Chuck said. "They're sealed with plastic."

"Of course you would," Peggy muttered, looking absolutely revolted.

Sheriff McKnight pulled Steve to his feet, not bothering to be gentle about it. "I'm going to lock this guy up."

She turned to Peggy. "Mind if I keep Jeremy here for another day? I need to call the coroner."

Peggy didn't look like she wanted to say yes, but no one was crazy enough to cross the sheriff at a time like this. "Of course. As long as you need."

Sheriff McKnight tossed a final glance my and Benji's way. "I know I said you needed to be gone by tomorrow, but given recent circumstances, I'll give you another day. After that, though, I never want to see either of you again."

"Fair enough," I said, ignoring her blatant lack of gratitude.

I didn't tell her about my promise to return with my children. I'd let that be a happy surprise for later.

23

Benji and I sat in the back of the tour truck, clinging to the roll bars and praying that the driver was as good as he thought he was. When we had signed up for the ghost town tour, I'd thought it would be a relaxing drive through the mountains and along old abandoned train tracks, discovering ruined remains of towns that had been vacant for decades.

No one had told us about the narrow dirt road that hugged the mountain, a steep drop-off on the other side. Or that we'd be in a vehicle that was completely open to the elements, the roll bar being the only thing that could protect us if the driver drove just a little too far to the right —the vehicle was so wide, it already took up most of the road. And if someone driving in the opposite direction thought they were going to be able to pass us? Forget it. We'd be at a standstill.

"Maybe we don't need to return with the kids," I shouted to Benji, trying to be heard over the wind as we bounced along. I pulled in long breaths, trying to calm my heart.

It didn't work.

Benji pulled me in for a side hug and then spoke directly in my ear. "Look at that mountain," he said, pointing to a beautiful mountain that towered over us—it still had snow at the top, even though we were coming close to the end of summer. "It's bigger than anything I've ever seen in my life. And at the base, see those old buildings?"

Benji was reminding me why we were here. And he was distracting me, helping me focus on something other than the narrow road we were on.

I loved so many things about Benji, but this was one of the reasons I'd chosen to marry him. Yes, he was good-looking and hilarious, and he was amazing with my kids. But this ability of his to see the bigger picture and take all of life in—it helped me to refocus my anxiety and broaden my vision.

And the view really was breathtaking. I'd almost missed the sprawl of green valley that surrounded us, followed by the transition to the mountain range. I'd almost missed the old, dilapidated buildings that had been constructed right along the mountain's base, as if they'd been using the mountains for protection. That was Benji's superpower—helping me not miss out on life because I couldn't get out of my own way.

However this honeymoon had gone—and I had to be honest, it hadn't gone well—I didn't regret a thing. The sheriff's focus had been so narrow, she never would have suspected her own deputy, and it was because of Benji and me that Seth and Amy were back in their saloon.

Phineas and Chuck had been arrested for their part in moving the body, as well as helping hide the stolen goods. They wouldn't be locked up for long, though—nothing compared to what Steve was about to go through.

That part of it did cast a bit of a cloud over the remaining time that Benji and I had on our honeymoon— I felt for Chuck. His friendship with Phineas had been so strong that he had been willing to hide a body to protect his friend. That level of devotion—I wanted to believe that if things all went sideways, I would hide a body for Benji. That was how strong I wanted this marriage to be.

I squeezed Benji's hand, then turned to face him. "Would you hide a body for me?"

To Benji's credit, he didn't look at all surprised by the question, and he instead smiled, then kissed me.

He then turned back to the scenery that was constantly unfolding before us, using one hand to hold on to the roll bar and keep himself from flying out of the bouncing vehicle.

He never answered me directly, but I took that as a *yes*.

And I leaned back into him, completely happy.

EPILOGUE

ONE YEAR LATER

I pulled in a long breath, relishing the salty air. This was the first time either Benji or I had ever been to the ocean, and the way the water stretched out in front of us until it disappeared beyond the horizon—it was overwhelming.

"I can't believe how big it is," I said, my gaze never leaving the ocean. The sun had just started to set, and it cast a pink glow over everything. I never wanted to leave.

"I know what you mean," Lilly said, her camera already out. "This is how I spend most of my evenings—just staring at the water. Sometimes I forget to even take the picture." She glanced at me. "I'm glad you chose here for our family vacation."

"Well, it hasn't been the same since you and Flash moved away, and we wanted to see what it was like," I said.

Benji stepped behind me and wrapped his arms around my waist. "Well worth it."

"Where I live, it's nothing like this," Flash said. "California is a big state, and you happened to pick the smallest, most idyllic town on the whole coast. When Lilly says she visits the ocean every night, it's next to some high rises, and she's standing on a rocky outcrop."

"That doesn't make it less beautiful," Lilly said. "It's just a different way of looking at the same ocean—it's exactly what photography is supposed to be."

"I'm just saying, Mom and Benji are going to get the wrong idea about what our life is like out here in California. It's fast-paced, and it's hard, and I don't get the luxury of visiting the beach anytime I want."

Lilly snorted. "When you have a day off, you choose not to visit the beach. You do what you've always done—sign up for some crazy coding competition that's at three a.m. because it's being hosted in a country on the other side of the world."

Flash raised a shoulder. "Hey, it pays the bills."

If by 'paying the bills' he meant that he made triple what any of us made, and he got to have fun while doing it.

I tore my gaze from the ocean and took in my two children. They'd grown a lot since moving out on their own—

matured. Mostly. It was more like an increase in confidence, like they were capable of taking on the world, and they didn't need their mom holding their hands while doing it.

I was proud of them, if not a little sad at not being needed anymore.

As I stood there, soaking in the moment, two older women approached us. A cat trotted ahead of them, restrained by a leash, and they had to pull the cat back.

"You picked a beautiful spot," one of them said to us. She had bright pink hair, and it made me a little jealous. I wished I could get away with something like that. Maybe when I was their age, I could.

"I can't get over how gorgeous this entire area is," I said, then turned back to the view.

"Of course, if you go further down the beach, you'll be able to join the rest of Starlight Ridge for the sunset stroll," she continued. "You can see that they are starting to light the bonfires, and the food will be showing up shortly."

Flash perked up at that. "Food?"

The other woman nodded. "Hot dogs and s'mores, with some fried fish thrown in for good measure."

Lilly wrinkled her nose. "I'll stick with the hot dogs and s'mores."

The pink-haired woman gave her a wink. "I'm with you on that one. Never been one to like seafood." She pulled on the leash to stop the cat, who was trying to break free to chase a seagull. "Skittles, on the other hand, is always up for fish."

Flash bent down to pet the cat, scratching it behind the ears. "Skittles has good taste."

"You here on vacation?" the pink-haired woman asked.

I nodded. "Yes. We're visiting from New Mexico."

The woman's eyes lit up. "Really. I used to live in New Mexico—it's a wonderful state." She then stuck on a hand. "I'm Jo Darby. Nice to make your acquaintance."

The other woman nodded, though her gaze was more guarded. "I'm her sister, Dottie."

"You can sit with us," Jo said, herding us toward the other end of the beach, where we saw people starting to set out their folding chairs.

"I don't know—" I said, sharing an anxious look with Benji. I had been thinking we'd take in the sunset for a little bit, then head to the bed and breakfast. I was exhausted from the long drive.

Benji took the hint and turned to the ladies. "We appreciate the offer, but maybe another time."

The pink-haired woman, Jo, raised the bag she was carrying and gave it a little shake. "Are you sure? We brought pastries from our bakery—they're quite well known in these parts. And they've only killed one person. Maybe two. But neither was our fault."

Her sister swatted her on the arm. "Don't tell them that. You'll scare them off."

Jo laughed. "I doubt it. Not when we make the best eclairs and madeleines on the West Coast."

And that was all it took for my kids to follow these two old women and their cat, like geriatric Pied Pipers, across the beach and to the sunset stroll.

"Do you think she was kidding?" I whispered to Benji, feeling we had no choice but to follow them. "About their pastries killing people, I mean."

"Of course she was kidding. Can you imagine those two women killing anyone?" He laughed at the idea of it.

Maybe not. But after what we'd experienced over the years, nothing surprised me anymore.

The way they'd already lured my children with their promise of food, I'd need to keep a close eye on those two for the remainder of our vacation.

The End

CHOOSE YOUR OWN ADVENTURE: MYSTERY OR ROMANCE

MADDIE SWALLOWS MYSTERIES:

New Mexican Cozy Mystery

Dead Before Dinner

Dead Upon Arrival

Dead Before I Do

Dead Among Stars

Dead by Design

Dead in the Dark

Dead Without a Hitch

Dead by the Outlaw's Noose

Dead in Starlight Ridge

SEASIDE FRENCH PATISSERIE MYSTERIES

Death and Dacquoise

Poison and Pudding

Bullets and Beignets

Murder and Madeleines

BORROWING AMOR: New Mexican Romance

Borrowing Amor

Borrowing Love

Borrowing a Fiancé

Borrowing a Billionaire

Borrowing Kisses

Borrowing Second Chances

STARLIGHT RIDGE: Beach Romance

Diving into Love

Resisting Love

Starlight Love

Building on Love

Winning his Love

Returning to Love

Fearless Love

ABOUT THE AUTHOR

Kat Bellemore is the author of both the Borrowing Amor small town romance series and the Maddie Swallows cozy mystery series. Deciding to have New Mexico as the setting for these series was an easy choice, considering its amazing sunsets, blue skies and tasty green chile. That, and she currently lives there with her husband and two cute kids. They hope to one day add a dog to the family, but for now, the native animals of the desert will have to do. Though, Kat wouldn't mind ridding the world of scorpions and centipedes. They're just mean.